THE BILLIONAIRE'S HOMECOMING

THE SHERBROOKES OF NEWPORT BOOK 11

CHRISTINA TETREAULT

CHAPTER 1

"MISSION CONTROL to space shuttle Jen, do you read me? I repeat, do you read me?"

Jennifer Wallace blinked and looked up at her sister, Kristen. "Sorry. Did you ask me something?"

Kristen nodded and held up a tomato. "I've asked you three times if you want tomatoes on your sandwich. Where were you?"

"Thinking. And no thanks, I'll skip the tomatoes today." She should've stayed home this afternoon, but she'd thought a change of scenery and some company would keep her thoughts off her upcoming meeting.

At the counter, Kristen put the finishing touches on their lunches and then called in Bella, Jen's niece, and her friend who was over for the afternoon. "Why don't you girls eat these on the deck," Kristen said, handing each girl a paper plate. "If you're still hungry later, we have ice cream in the freezer and peanut butter cookies."

Neither girl argued, and they quickly disappeared back outside.

"Do you want to talk about whatever has you so distracted?

Maybe I can help." Kristen set down their sandwiches and an unopened bag of barbecue-flavored potato chips, their favorite flavor.

There was no way Kristen or anyone else could help, but maybe talking about it would get it out of her head for a bit. "Do you remember me telling you about Brett, the man I've been exchanging letters and texts with for the past year and a half?"

"Actually, it's been almost two years. We sent the first care boxes to Keith's unit at the start of our second year as Girl Scout leaders. This September will be our fourth year," Kristen said, referring to their older brother.

Jen ground her back molars together. She loved her sister, but the woman didn't understand the concept of approximation. Even in school she'd never been able to estimate the answer to a math problem. Nope, she had to get the exact answer. Jen, as well as perhaps everyone in the family, found it Kristen's most annoying characteristic. Often they teased her about it when it reared its ugly head—like now. This afternoon, Jen ignored it. Sometimes it was easier.

"But to answer your question, yes, I remember. You've talked so much about him I feel like I know him," Kristen said.

"I'm supposed to finally meet him this week after work."

Kristen tore open the chips and added a handful to her plate before passing the bag to Jen. "In a public place I hope."

Although really her adopted sister and only six months older, Kristen had always played the role of the protective big sister. "Yes, of course. We're meeting at Ambrosia."

"Awesome. What's the problem then? You're already half in love with the man. I'd think you'd be excited about finally meeting him face-to-face."

Unfortunately, her sister's assessment wasn't far from the truth. She'd never admit Kristen was right though. Kristen's belief that she was always correct no matter the topic was her sister's second-biggest flaw.

2

"Well, let's see," Jen said. "To start with, I'm about to sit down and have coffee with Brett Sherbrooke. You may have heard of his family. They own this small, insignificant hotel chain, but if you haven't, I'm sure you've heard of his uncle, President Sherbrooke. You know, the man who lives in the big white house on Pennsylvania Avenue and travels in Air Force One."

Her sister's mouth opened and closed several times. She'd had a similar reaction when she finally found out just whom she'd been corresponding with for months too.

"Wait, a minute. Back up." Kristen pointed a potato chip at her. "You never told me any of this before. Does Keith know?"

Since Brett and their brother had served together, Jen guessed he knew, although Keith had never mentioned it to her. "Probably, but I never asked him. I'm not even sure Keith knows Brett and I have been communicating all this time. I never told him. Did you?"

Kristen shook her head. "Why didn't you tell me before now? I mean it's not like you never talk about the man."

"At first I only knew his first name. Later, I thought it was just a coincidence his name was Brett Sherbrooke. A lot of people have the same name. I knew a guy at Northeastern named Anderson Brady, and he wasn't the actor."

"Fair enough. But you must have learned the truth long before this month. You've been writing to him for almost two years!"

Jen toyed with the napkin near her plate and nodded. "Yeah, but when I figured it out, he was halfway across the world in some place I can't even pronounce. It didn't seem like a big deal."

"How *did* you figure it out anyway? Did he actually tell you in an e-mail or something?"

She remembered very well the moment she put it together. "Not exactly. Last year he mentioned how disappointed he was that he wasn't going to make it to Providence for his cousin Trent's wedding."

Jen could accept there was more than one man in the world with the name Brett Sherbrooke. She couldn't accept there was more than one who also had a cousin named Trent living in Providence who was getting married.

"I see how you would've reached that conclusion. I would've too, but did you ever actually ask him? It might be a stretch, but he still might not be part of *that* Sherbrooke family."

"Oh, trust me he is. We exchanged pictures sometime last year, and I compared it to a picture I found on the internet taken at a fund-raiser a few years ago. In it he's standing with Jake and Trent Sherbrooke."

Kristen tapped her fingers on the table but didn't respond right away. While Jen waited for her sister's next question, and she knew there would be more, she started on her lunch.

Her sister's fingers stopped moving. "I'd be a little nervous too, but I don't see what the big deal is. You've never met in person, but it's not like you don't know the guy. The two of you have exchanged enough letters, e-mails, and texts to wallpaper my entire house. And you already know what he looks like, so you don't have to worry about finding some eighty-year-old man with warts waiting for you. I say relax, enjoy the afternoon, and see where things go."

Ah yes, they'd exchanged pictures, and there was the other problem that had been plaguing her thoughts ever since Brett said he was moving back to New England and would love to finally meet.

"Well, the whole picture thing is kind of part of the problem."

"I'm afraid to ask, but I will anyway," Kristen said.

Of course she would because this was her sister. And Kristen never held anything back. It was actually one of the things she loved about her. Kristen was always upfront and honest.

"Did you send him a picture of someone else?"

She'd briefly considered it, because at the time she hadn't expected to ever meet him. Kristen didn't need to know that small detail. "Of course not."

"Then what? Did you have one of those boudoir photo shoots done and then send him some sexy pictures?"

Really, Kristen knew her better than that, but evidently she wanted to give her a hard time this afternoon. "Get real. That's something you'd do and then give to Dan as a present."

"Did he tell you?" Her sister's face took on a slight pink hue.

"Your husband didn't tell me anything. But your face is right now. Did you really have one of those done?" For the moment their discussion of her upcoming meeting could take a back burner. This was way too good to pass up

The pink spread from Kristen's cheeks to her hairline, and she looked away. "I wanted to get him something different for his birthday. I'd read about them being *the thing* right now and figured what the heck. He's the only one who'll ever see them." She cleared her throat and met Jen's eyes again. "But let's get back to your story. It's more interesting."

She'd love to tease Kristen about the photo gift, but if she did, her sister would find some way to repay the favor later. "I sent Brett my favorite picture from Mom and Dad's fortieth anniversary party. You know, the one I had framed of you, me, and Keith together."

"It's a great picture of you. I don't see the problem."

"That's the problem right there. It's too good. It's not the real me. Before the party, we both went to the salon and had someone do our hair and makeup. Before he printed the picture, the photographer removed any blemishes. I never look the way I do in that photo." It was one of the reasons she'd had it framed in the first place.

Kristen waved a dismissive hand in her direction. "Jennifer, you're being absolutely ridiculous. You never wear your hair the way you did to the party, but otherwise you don't look any different in the picture than you normally do."

She had a mirror at home, and the reflection greeting her every morning did not resemble the person in the picture she'd sent Brett. Unfortunately, there wasn't much she could do about it now. So the way she saw it, she had two options: either meet Brett this week at Ambrosia, or cancel altogether. But canceling their meeting would probably also mean she'd have to stop corresponding with him—something she didn't want to do.

"I'm still not sure I should go."

"Come on, be serious. What's the worst thing that could happen? You talk and then you go home alone and never hear from him again. Truthfully, I don't see that happening. Not after all this time."

She couldn't argue with Kristen's logic. Her life wouldn't end if their meeting didn't go well. She'd be disappointed though, because like her sister said, she was already half in love with the man.

"And if it does happen, well, his loss, not yours. Besides, who knows, you might spend five minutes with the man and decide he's the biggest jerk who ever lived." Kristen touched her hand and gave it a squeeze. "Jen, go. Drink some coffee, talk, and see what happens."

Just because they'd never met face-to-face didn't mean she didn't know Brett well enough to know he wasn't a jerk.

"What's it going to be, sis? Finally meet the potential love of your life, or help me take Bella and her friends to their first concert. It's not sold out; I can still get you a ticket. I'll even order it before you leave today."

She loved her niece, but she had no desire to take Bella and her friends to their first concert. "Tough one. I can either have coffee with a gorgeous man or help supervise a group of nine- and ten-year-old girls." Jen pretended to weigh both options with her hands. "Thanks for the offer, sis, but this time I'll go the gorgeous man route."

~

BRETT FOLLOWED the GPS directions and took a left. Sprawling estates lined both sides of the street. He'd visited his cousin Callie's home in Connecticut only once despite numerous invites in the past. He hadn't planned on visiting today, but a stop there now would help break up his ride from Virginia to Massachusetts—a trip he'd started over eleven hours ago. And assuming he didn't hit any more traffic, he still had another three and a half hours to look forward to. Delays through Maryland and New Jersey had already tacked on several extra hours in the car, and he didn't know how much more he could handle. A short visit at his cousin's house would give him a chance to relax, stretch his legs, and hopefully avoid any weekend backups on the Mass Turnpike.

"You have arrived. Your destination is on the right," the GPS informed him.

After turning, he approached the security gate and pressed the intercom.

"Can I help you?" a male voice asked

"I'm here to see Callie and Dylan," Brett answered.

"Name, please."

"Brett."

"I'm sorry, there is no Brett on the guest list. I'll have to check with the Talbots."

Guest list? Damn, were Callie and Dylan having a party? "I'm her cousin," he added, not that he expected the individual to open the gate without speaking to either his cousin or her husband first.

"One moment please."

The intercom went silent, and Brett considered calling Callie rather than wait for whoever had answered to find her in the house. Before he got the chance, the gates opened. He didn't wait for any further invitation.

He drove down the long, winding driveway. When he reached the house, he found several other cars already parked there. The only one he recognized was his brother's car. All the others had out-of-state plates though, and since two were from Rhode Island, two were from Virginia, and another from New York, he assumed several of his family members were visiting. With so many relatives here, Brett had a feeling he'd be there longer than he'd originally planned.

Before he had a chance to ring the doorbell, the front door opened and a petite woman stepped toward him.

"I can't believe you're here." Callie hugged him before he could manage a simple hello. "Everyone's going to be so surprised when they see you."

Brett hugged her back. "Having a party?"

"Don't worry, it's only family." She closed the door behind him as she spoke. "Well, Lauren and her husband, Nate, are here too, but they're like family."

He'd never met Callie's best friend, but he'd heard her talk about Lauren and her husband. Callie listed the other family members there as she led him through the house.

"Look who's here," she said, stepping outside before him.

All conversations stopped, and every head turned his way. Even the toddlers playing seemed to pause and look at him. Just as suddenly everyone started talking at once.

"Did you finally decide to go AWOL?" his brother, Curt, asked, coming over and giving him a hug and slap on the back.

"Nah, the Army decided they'd had enough of him and kicked him to the curb," Trent, one of his many cousins present, said, giving him a hug as well.

Brett accepted the lemonade Callie handed him and took a sip before answering. "Thought I'd stop and visit on my way home. If I'd known you two were here, I would've kept on going."

His younger brother shrugged and rejoined the woman he'd been sitting with. She'd been with Curt at Kiera and Gray's wedding in June too, although he hadn't spoken much to her. He hadn't had a chance. Before the ceremony even started, they'd left because she had an emergency at home. He hadn't spoken with his brother since then, so he didn't know what the emergency had been or how it had turned out.

"In case you don't remember him, Taylor, this grouch is my brother, Brett," Curt said to the woman next to him.

Ignoring his brother's comment, he approached Curt's girlfriend. "It's nice to see you again." Brett smiled and held out his hand.

Shaking his hand, Taylor smiled back. "Likewise."

"So where have you been?" Callie asked.

He watched the toddlers who were playing with a young girl he didn't recognize. He hadn't seen any of his cousins' children in several months, but it was easy to pick out James, Callie and Dylan's son. He had dark brown hair like Callie and Dylan, and blue-gray eyes. Figuring out which child belonged to Trent and which belonged to Jake was another story. Both had the trademark Sherbrooke blue eyes, a trait his brother possessed as well, and dirty-blond hair. It didn't help that Kendrick, Trent's son, and Garrett, Jake's son, were only three months apart in age.

"Nowhere," he answered. For the moment, he gave up trying to figure out which boy belonged to which cousin and turned his attention to the young girl. She looked to be about seven or so. Since he knew she didn't belong to any of his cousins, she had to be related to either Callie's friend Lauren or Curt's girlfriend. Curt hadn't mentioned his girlfriend had any children, but the girl didn't resemble Lauren or husband in the least either.

"Two seconds ago you said you were on your way back to Virginia," Trent said.

"He's experiencing memory problems. It happens a lot to old people," Curt said.

If not for the children present, he'd tell his brother just where he could shove his comment.

"He's not old, Curt," the unknown girl said, looking back at his brother before he could come up with a suitable non-explicit response to Curt's insult.

Taylor laughed. "Reese, Curt's only teasing his brother."

"But he is older than me," Curt added.

Mystery solved. The girl belonged with Taylor. He'd have to ask Curt later why he hadn't told him his new girlfriend had a daughter. "Wrong. I said I was on my way home. I never mentioned Virginia."

Other than Dad, Uncle Warren, and his friend Jen, no one knew his plans. He'd held off on sharing them with anyone else, even Mom, in case something unexpected happened. With everything on track, he saw no reason to keep quiet any longer.

"Then you're going to see Mom and Dad?" Curt asked.

He hadn't thought of his parents' house as home in a long time. "No. I'm headed to North Salem," Brett answered. "I bought a house there about a year ago."

"Really?" Jake asked.

Brett thought he'd told his cousin, but evidently he hadn't. "Yeah, your brother-in-law checks on it once a month or so for me."

He'd met Sean O'Brien, Jake's brother-in-law, at his cousin's house not long after Jake got married. They'd hit it off and become friends. When he'd decided to buy a place in North Salem where both Jake's brother-in-law and mother-in-law lived, Sean had offered to check in on it and let him know if any problems developed. Thankfully, none ever had.

"Sean never said anything to me," Jake said before turning to his wife. "Did he tell you?"

Charlie shook her head. "Nope. Where in town is it?"

Charlie had grown up in North Salem and made regular trips back to visit her family whenever she could.

"Union Street. Not far from the police station." Since he'd known the house would be vacant for at least a year, he'd figured owning a home virtually across the street from a police station was a bonus.

"My friend Jessie and her husband live on Union Street," Charlie said, picking up the little boy now standing near her, solving the mystery of which toddler was Jake's son.

Brett hadn't spent enough time at the house to meet any of his neighbors. In the time he'd owned it, he'd only stayed there a handful of nights, the most recent being when he'd come home for his cousin's wedding in June.

"How long are you staying up here this time?" Curt asked. "If you have time, come up and visit us. North Salem isn't far from Pelham."

"Permanently." He'd spent a fair amount of time preparing for this transition, but saying the word still felt strange.

Jake laughed at him. "Nice one. You almost had me. You went a little too far though. Everyone here knows you didn't retire from the Army. It's stuck with you for life. What are you really doing up here this weekend?"

Fair enough. Since the day he entered West Point, he'd never let on he intended to do more with his life than serve his country. And until the past two or so years, he hadn't considered it himself. "I didn't retire, but I'm no longer on active duty either. If I'm needed, they can call me up, but I don't see it happening."

"You're serious?" Curt asked, still sounding suspicious.

Brett nodded. "Affirmative. I plan to run for Senator Marshall's seat next year."

Few people knew the longtime United States Senator from Massachusetts didn't intend to run for reelection when his term ended the following year. However, since Senator Marshall happened to be good friends with his uncles and dad, he'd learned of the man's plan more than a year ago. "That's why I bought the house in North Salem when I did."

"Dad mentioned Richard wasn't going to run again," Curt said. "Half expected him to suggest I move back to Massachusetts and run for it. Not that I ever would, but we both know that wouldn't stop Dad from trying."

It was no secret Jonathan Sherbrooke still wanted his sons to follow the same path so many Sherbrooke males had been taking for years. For a long time, Dad had been content his younger son worked in the financial world at least. However, Curt's recent decision to leave his position at Nichols Investment to be a full-time author baffled the man.

"Let me see if I've got this. You're moving to North Salem and running for Richard Marshall's Senate seat next year?" Jake asked.

His cousin still didn't sound as if he believed anything Brett had told him. And Brett understood Jake's lack of acceptance. In many ways they were a lot alike. Neither had followed the path their fathers had wanted them to, and neither had ever exhibited any interest in entering politics. Trent had always been the one they expected to follow that particular Sherbrooke tradition.

"Did you take a blow to the head recently?" Curt asked before Brett answered Jake. "You detest politics."

His brother was wrong on that front. He didn't hate politics. Rather, he disliked most of the politicians serving in Washington. Brett saw that as a big distinction.

"I think it's a great idea," Callie said before Trent or another of his cousins who hadn't chimed in yet could give him a hard time too. "Let me know if I can help."

"You're serious," Curt said.

"I already have a list of potential campaign managers from Uncle Warren and Dad."

Trent and Dylan, Callie's husband, exchanged a look. "If

Marty Phillips is on the list, ignore him and keep looking," Trent said.

"Trent's right," Dylan added.

He'd scanned the list quickly but didn't recall if the man had been mentioned or not. But he trusted Trent's and Dylan's judgment. If his cousin and his friend thought he should avoid Marty Phillips, he would. There were plenty of names on the list anyway.

"Anyone you recommend, Trent?" Brett asked.

Prior to his marriage, Trent had planned to run for the US Senate himself. According to Curt, their cousin had even hired a campaign manager. Before any serious campaigning could get underway, Trent had changed his mind and soon after announced his engagement. However, it wasn't a secret Trent still planned to enter politics someday.

Trent reached down and grabbed the pink plastic pig his son had sent flying under his chair. "I'd go with anyone Uncle Warren suggested except Marty Phillips," he answered, handing the toy back to Kendrick, who walked back to the farmhouse he was playing with.

He'd look over the list, talk to Dad and maybe his uncles too, and do some research. It wasn't like he had to make a decision this week or anything.

ALTHOUGH HE FOUND SPENDING time with his family enjoyable, he was anxious to get home. So when Callie invited him to spend the night, he turned down her offer. Pulling over for a second time since leaving her house, he wished he hadn't. The rain had started the moment he crossed the Connecticut–Massachusetts border. At first it had been little more than a soft drizzle. It had quickly changed to a downpour as the winds picked up. A dazzling lightning storm soon followed. He'd been forced to pull over into the breakdown lane the first time visibility became nonexistent, outside of Grafton. He'd sat there for a solid ten minutes before the rain let up enough to see again.

Brett switched on the car's hazard lights, although considering the visibility out there, he didn't think any approaching vehicles would even see them. Picking up his cell phone, he opened the weather app. He didn't like what he saw. According to the screen, the storm was moving toward North Salem rather than away from it. He'd be dealing with it the rest of his trip home.

He'd heard his cell phone beep while driving. Pulled over for the moment anyway, he checked the text message.

Call me as soon as you get a chance. The message from Dad immediately sent up red flags.

Dad never asked him to call, and they already had plans to meet this week. If Dad was requesting a call tonight, something must be wrong. He'd seen Nana less than two months ago at his cousin's wedding. She'd looked as healthy and energetic as always despite her advanced years. Had something happened to her or Mom?

Before calling, he checked his watch. It was close to one in the morning. If he called back now, he risked waking his parents. Instead he hit reply and typed back a message. If Dad remained awake, he'd answer, and if not, he'd try again later in the morning. Brett held the phone and waited.

The rain pounding the windshield gradually subsided, and Brett could once again see the road. Tossing the cell phone onto the passenger seat, he got back underway. No reply from Dad either meant the man was asleep or too busy. He'd have to wait to find out what was going on and hope everyone he cared about was okay.

CHAPTER 2

HE FLIPPED up the switch on the wall, but the bedroom light remained off. He'd expected as much this morning. It'd been out last night when he got here too. Considering all the downed trees and power lines he passed on his way through town, he assumed it'd be some time before he had power back. Perhaps having an empty refrigerator this morning wasn't the worst thing in the world.

Before leaving the bedroom, he grabbed his cell phone off the nightstand and checked for any new messages. He'd never heard back from Dad or received any message from anyone else before falling asleep.

Nothing. Damn. Brett looked at his watch. He'd wait a little longer before he called Dad. Until then he'd check the property for any damage. Something big had been hit last night. It had woken him. When no large tree landed in his bedroom or any other part of the house, he dismissed it as something to look into when the sun came up.

Brett entered the empty living room. Tomorrow the little furniture he did own would arrive, but at some point he'd need more. The condo he'd lived in for the past couple years was much smaller than this place. When his younger sister had visited during his last stay here, she'd offered to do all the furniture shopping and decorating for him. He hadn't even considered Leah's offer before turning it down. While he appreciated the gesture, he'd seen the museum she called a home. He didn't need or want her turning this place into its duplicate, no matter how convenient it would be to let her handle it all.

Opening the door, he stepped outside and swore. Something big had come down all right, and now it was lying across his driveway. Until he got rid of the tree, he wouldn't be getting his car out of the garage.

Be happy it didn't land on your car, he reminded himself. With no power, he'd been forced to fight with the manual release on the garage door when he arrived. The evidence blocking his driveway proved the extra effort had been worth it despite the aggravation.

He moved off the porch so he could get a better look at what he was dealing with. The front yard was covered with branches and leaves from the many trees in his yard and perhaps his neighbors' yards too. However, he didn't think the tree currently taking a nap in his driveway was actually one of his. He had a decent idea of where his property line was, and he had a feeling this tree belonged to his neighbor. Not that it made much of a difference if the tree belonged to him or not at the moment. It was still residing in his yard and complicating his life.

Thanks to Mother Nature, it appeared as though he'd be meeting his neighbors sooner than he expected. Before he went over to talk to them about it, he'd check out the rest of his property and see if he had any other major problems to deal with this morning.

Brett walked around the right side of the house and through the gate into the backyard. Several large limbs littered this part of the property, but with a chainsaw, all could be cut into smaller pieces. Later in the winter he could burn the wood in the fireplace. He passed by the in-ground pool. He'd considered having it opened earlier in the month so it'd be ready when he moved in. Considering the debris filling his yard, he was glad he'd never gotten around to finding a pool company to do it. With the summer more than half over anyway, he might not even bother now.

Pleased the property hadn't suffered any significant damage, he exited the backyard through the gate by the garage and found a man around his age standing in the driveway and examining the downed tree. When the stranger glanced up, he waved at Brett.

"Morning. I would've knocked if I'd known someone was here," the man said as Brett approached. "Mack Ellsbury, I live next door." The man pointed to the house on the left. "You must be Sean's friend."

Brett stopped and extended his hand. "Brett Sherbrooke. I arrived early this morning."

"Doesn't look like this tree caused any damage. I'll work on getting it out of your way. My wife wanted to get rid of it last fall so she could plant a flower garden. Looks like she got her wish."

"I'll give you a hand," Brett answered. If they worked together, the tree would be off his property sooner.

"Appreciate the help. How 'bout a cup of coffee before we get started?"

"You've got power?"

Mack shook his head. "No, a generator. I had it installed last year. We tend to lose power often in the winter."

Perhaps having a generator installed before the winter months arrived belonged on his to-do list. "Coffee sounds good. I've got a quick phone call to make, and I'll be right over."

Brett waited for his neighbor to leave before calling his dad. The phone rang several times before Jonathan Sherbrooke answered.

"What's wrong? Are Mom and Nana okay?" Brett asked before his dad managed to say anything more than a hello. "Did something happen to Leah?"

"Everyone is fine. Nothing is wrong," Dad assured him.

Considering the message Dad sent him, he hadn't expected him to sound so calm this morning. "Your text insinuated otherwise."

"I should've been clearer. I apologize," Dad said. "Have you been following the news at all?"

"Not really. I've been too busy with my move back here. Why? What happened?"

"Neil Brown passed away last week."

He knew of the longtime senator. Probably everyone in the country had heard of him. Neil Brown was the longest-serving senator in United States history. Brett also knew the man's health had been declining over the past year. However, he'd never met the man.

"You realize what it means, don't you?" Dad asked.

Yeah, Massachusetts was now short one senator in Washington.

"The state is going to have to hold a special election to fill his seat. He had another three years in office. The governor announced the dates for the election yesterday. The primary will be held November 7 and the election will be six weeks later," Dad said before Brett commented. "I discussed it with your uncles yesterday. Rather than wait and run for Richard's seat next year, we all agree you should try for Brown's now."

Brett processed Dad's statement. He had a well-thought-out strategy, and he'd already executed the first half of it. Entering the special election and running for Brown's Senate seat would mean tossing the rest of it out the window and starting over.

"You're a Massachusetts resident again and living in the state. There's no reason to wait until next year."

Dad was right on both accounts. He'd changed his residency status when he'd been up for Gray's wedding. While some may not agree with it, Massachusetts didn't require a candidate to have lived in the state for a specific amount of time before running for a seat in the United States Senate. It only required an individual be an inhabitant of the state when elected. According to his driver's license and voter registration, he was a resident again and had been since June.

"I need to think about it," Brett answered.

"What is there to think about? You've been positioning yourself for this for over a year. Getting you on the ballot for the primary should be a piece of cake. When we meet this week, we can discuss the particulars and get the ball rolling."

Dad had been disappointed in Brett when he failed to follow the path of most Sherbrooke males. He'd never said that, but it had been very clear. When Brett told him his plan to leave active duty and enter politics, the man had all but done a victory dance. This morning Brett wasn't surprised by Dad's insistence he change his timetable and jump into politics sooner rather than later.

"Give me twenty-four hours to think it over. I'll let you know." Regardless of what a good idea Dad and his uncles thought it was, he wasn't going to jump headfirst into a decision without examining it from every position.

Brett finished the call and crossed the yard. As he rang his neighbors' doorbell, visions of hot coffee filled his thoughts.

The sound of a barking dog responded moments before Mack opened the door. "Don't worry. Socks is friendly." Mack pointed to the dog near his feet. "C'mon in."

Brett followed his neighbor and the dog through the living room where an enormous dollhouse stood near the fireplace, indicating Mack had at least one child.

"Brett, this is my wife, Jessie," Mack said when they entered the kitchen.

The woman at the stove looked ready to give birth right then and there.

"And my daughter, Grace." Mack ruffled the girl's hair before grabbing a mug from a cabinet.

Brett recalled his conversation with his cousin's wife yesterday. Charlie had mentioned that her friend Jessie and her husband lived on Union Street. "You're not by any chance friends with Charlie Sherbrooke?"

Jessie flipped a pancake on the stove and then looked over at him. "Charlie was my maid of honor." She flipped another pancake before she spoke again. "Sean told us a friend of his bought the house next door. When Mack told me your name this morning, I assumed you must be one of Jake's cousins."

"Guilty. But try not to hold it against me," Brett said, accepting the coffee Mack held out.

Jessie laughed and rubbed her lower back. "Yeah, I wouldn't want to admit I was related to him either," she said good-naturedly.

"Jake danced with me at Jessie and Dad's wedding," Grace said, joining in the conversation.

For some reason the comment didn't surprise him.

"More than once," Jessie added. She refilled Grace's milk and went back to the stove. "The pancakes are almost done if you're hungry, Brett. There is more than enough here."

It'd been hours since he last ate, and he had absolutely nothing in his kitchen. If his neighbor was offering him breakfast, he wouldn't turn it down.

"Jessie makes the best pancakes," Grace said. "You'll love 'em."

"If they're the best, I can't say no. Thank you."

～

RELAX, you practically know him already. Jen repeated the

sentence over again in her head. She'd been more or less repeating the same words in some form or another since she agreed to tonight's meeting. Despite the numerous times and many variations, they were not helping.

The cell phone in her shoulder bag dinged as she pushed open the door to Ambrosia Pastry Shop and Café on Benefit Street. Before checking it, she scouted out the popular café. In the morning and afternoon, the place was normally packed with customers of all ages. With the workday over for many, she had her selection of open tables and booths.

Today she wanted a seat with a good view of the door. Since it would only be the two of them, she walked past the tables designed for groups and settled on a small booth near the windows. From there she could see the front entrance and also part of the sidewalk leading up to the café.

Sliding behind the table, she pulled out her cell phone.

The short text from Kristen came as no big surprise. *Relax and have fun tonight. Let me know how it goes.*

Jen responded with an *ok* and pulled up her e-mail. As usual she was early. She couldn't help it. While some people were perpetually late for meetings and get-togethers, she had the opposite problem, especially when she was doing something out of her regular routine. Meeting the man she'd been communicating with for almost two years certainly fit into the way-out-of-her-daily-routine category. She just hoped Brett was on time. Her deodorant might not hold up if he showed up ten or twenty minutes late. As it was, she wasn't confident it would last the fifteen minutes until he was supposed to arrive, and she'd even put more on before leaving the office.

The majority of e-mails clogging her inbox were either spam messages or ads from her favorite stores. She deleted them all without opening any first. She did open the one claiming a Nigerian prince wanted to give her five million dollars, but only because she found those e-mails and the ones she got claiming she'd won some foreign lottery amusing. She never responded to them, of course, but every once in a while she wanted to send them a message back, thanking them and asking what she had to do to claim the money just so she could see how long she could keep the game going.

With the temporary distraction gone, she checked her watch. Phooey, she'd managed to waste less than five minutes. Now what? She looked over her shoulder at the cases filled with various baked goods. Unfortunately, when she got nervous, rather than lose her appetite, she ate. Jen knew she wouldn't be disappointed with anything she might order here because she often stopped in and picked up a spinach pie or a calzone for lunch. Ambrosia's biscotti and tiramisu were divine as well. However, today the last thing she needed was to eat and then get a piece of food stuck between her teeth. Talk about making a terrible first impression. Tea or coffee should be fairly safe though, assuming she didn't spill it all over her white blouse. Another embarrassment she could do without tonight.

Jen left her sweater on the table. She had the perfect location in the café and didn't want to lose it while she ordered. Before joining the short line at the counter, she grabbed the newest copy of *The Star Report*. This week a picture of actor Anderson Brady took up the cover. She didn't read the popular magazine often, but it had great crossword puzzles. She could work on this week's while she waited, killing whatever time she had left.

"What can I get for you today?" Chloe, according to her name tag, asked. Until recently the woman had been a permanent fixture at the café. Jen hadn't seen the employee in a few months, and she'd assumed the woman had left.

Setting down the magazine, she considered her drink options before deciding to keep it simple tonight. "Large dark roast with milk and two sugars." While Chloe prepared her order, she spoke again. "I haven't seen you here all summer." There was no one in line behind her, so a brief conversation wouldn't hold up anything.

Chloe set down the coffee. "I finished my degree back in January and took a position at Gatekeeper Gaming. I only fill in when they need someone, like tonight."

She wasn't into gaming, but she'd heard of the video game company located downtown. "Well, it's nice to see you. Have a good night." Jen paid for her magazine and coffee and returned to her booth.

Okay, let's see how much time I can kill with this. She flipped the magazine over and opened to the crossword puzzle. She filled in ten answers before glancing at the door when the hands on her watch read six o'clock. On cue the door opened, but the college-age man with the shaggy hair and well-worn T-shirt wasn't the man she wanted.

Glancing down again, she read the clue for seven down, *Location of the 2012 summer Olympics.* She never watched the games, however, the answer contained only six letters and the third one was an *N*. Jen remembered sometime in the past decade the Olympics had been held in London. London contained six letters.

Jen filled in the boxes and jumped to the next clue, *Second United States President.* "Too easy," she mumbled and moved her pen toward the puzzle boxes again. The voice in her head suddenly telling her to look up stopped her from doing anything else. Squeezing her eyes shut for a moment, she took a deep breath, counted to ten, and looked up toward the entrance.

Wow. The thought zipped through her head the moment she saw the dark-haired man standing there. *This was a first-class bad idea* quickly followed.

The man had looked handsome in both the picture he'd sent her and the one she'd found on the internet. The individual standing at the entrance now went beyond handsome—not to mention way out of her league. In fact, she wouldn't be shocked if after seeing her, Brett pretended he hadn't and then walked right back out without as much as a hello first.

Across the café, Brett opened the door for a woman leaving. Jen held her breath and waited for him to follow the customer outside and back down the sidewalk. Instead he let the door close behind him and headed straight for her booth, catching the attention of several women and one man along the way.

Slipping her hands under the table, she wiped her damp palms on her skirt and put what she hoped resembled a smile on her face.

"Jen," Brett said. There wasn't a hint of uncertainty in his voice. "I hope you haven't been waiting long. There was an accident on North Main Street. I ended up parking in a garage over there and walking here."

"I arrived a few minutes ago." He didn't need to know she'd been there for a solid fifteen minutes, half of which she spent contemplating whether she should leave or not. "Please have a seat. Or would you like a coffee? I can go order you one. Or I can order you something to eat. The food here is great if you're hungry." *Great, keep rambling like an idiot.*

He cocked an eyebrow. She always wondered how people did that. She couldn't even wink, never mind control her eyebrows.

"I haven't even sat down and you're trying to get away from me," Brett said.

Shoot. One of these days she'd learn to shut up. "I only meant…," she began, hoping to clarify her previous statement. The smile tugging at his lips stopped her. "You're just giving me a hard time, aren't you?"

"Affirmative. But if you don't mind, I will grab a coffee and come right back. Can I get you anything?"

Jen held up her coffee. "All set for now, I ordered one when I arrived."

She resisted the urge to turn and watch him walk to the

counter. The women a few tables over were not as disciplined. She didn't blame them. Put in their position, she might have done the same thing. When it came to looks, there was nothing average about Brett Sherbrooke, a fact that came as no surprise to her. Over the years, she'd seen pictures of his various relatives in magazines and on the internet. Every single one of them put the rest of the population to shame. Even Brett's uncle, President Warren Sherbrooke, was an extremely handsome man. And as much as she enjoyed looking at handsome men, a part of her wished the man ordering a coffee was a little less drop-dead gorgeous. Someone who looked like him didn't get involved with plain Janes like her.

"Couldn't resist," Brett said. He placed a tray with a cannoli and steaming coffee on the table. "They make the best cannoli anywhere."

Under the table, she uncrossed and then crossed her legs again. "If you say so. I can't stand them no matter who makes them."

"Don't let my cousin hear you say that. He'll ban you from his house. They're Trent's favorite. His mother-in-law keeps him well supplied with them."

She never planned on meeting Trent Sherbrooke or any of Brett's other relatives, so she wasn't worried about being banned from anywhere. Actually, she wasn't even sure she'd see Brett again. After tonight they might very well just go back to exchanging friendly e-mails and text messages. Perhaps they wouldn't even do that anymore.

"It's the filling. I hate ricotta cheese," she said.

Both his eyebrows went up this time. "And you're just telling me this now? I don't know if we can be friends."

This time she knew he was only giving her a hard time. "Consider this your warning. If you ever come to my house for dinner, don't expect lasagna, ravioli, or baked stuffed shells. They don't cross my kitchen table."

Brett raised his mug toward his mouth. While he sipped his coffee, she took the opportunity to study his bare forearms. They were well tanned, like his face, and muscular. Her eyes traveled higher. His shirtsleeves covered his upper arms but didn't hide his chiseled biceps.

"How do you feel about pizza?" he asked, lowering his mug again.

She suspected her waistline answered his question for her. "Perhaps my all-time favorite food. I think I could eat it every day."

He exhaled loudly. "For a moment I thought I'd have to leave. But as long as you like pizza, I can associate with you."

The humor Brett was displaying now was the same she picked up on in his many letters and messages. For the first time since stepping out of the shower this morning, she relaxed. True, this was their first face-to-face meeting, but she knew this man. Considered him a good friend.

BRETT WATCHED the smile form on Jen's face. *Mission successful.*

He'd spotted her the moment he walked in Ambrosia. Even with her head down making it difficult to see her face, he'd recognized the strawberry-blonde hair from her picture. When she did look up, her expression told him everything he needed to know. For some unknown reason, she was nervous. Immediately, getting her to relax became his main objective. Judging by the smile on her face, he'd succeeded.

"Ah, but what if we don't like the same kind?" she asked. "Then what?"

"Not possible. I've never tried a pizza I didn't like." Brett reached for his cannoli. He'd had a late lunch with his parents, but in his opinion there was always room for dessert. Especially anything this café made. He'd lived in a lot of different places, but he'd never found a bakery that came close to this one.

Jen put an elbow on the table and rested her chin on her knuckles. "Even one with clams and peppers on it?"

"Never tried it, but I'm game. Name the day and time and we'll get one together."

When they first started exchanging letters, he expected it would last a couple months and then stop. However, the letters and e-mails continued. When he came back from his last deployment several months ago, they'd added sending text messages to their modes of communication. When he'd finalized his plans to move back to New England, she'd been one of the few people he told.

"I'll check my calendar and get back to you." She reached for her coffee and took a sip. "So, are you all moved into your new house?"

"More or less. My furniture arrived yesterday. I've got a few boxes to unpack. It won't take me long." He'd never been one for unnecessary items, a useful characteristic considering the number of times he'd moved.

"I hate packing and unpacking. I might stay where I am until I die," Jen said.

Her comment suggested she'd moved around a fair amount herself. She'd never said as much, but he'd assumed she always lived in Rhode Island.

"When do you start at Homeland Security?" she asked.

When he'd accepted the position to work as a contractor in Homeland Security's cyber division, she'd been the first person he told. Before today, the only other person besides her to know had been Dad. He'd finally shared the news with Mom this afternoon. "Monday."

"Great timing. The rest of the week is supposed to be beautiful. Perfect beach weather." She smiled, the expression changing her face from just pretty to beautiful. "If you get bored and want to fill in for me at work, I'll trade with you. My tan needs some work." She held out her arm, which compared to his skin remained pale.

"If you want to keep the promotion you got a few months ago, you don't want me doing your work." He eyed the guy approaching the counter. His head was shaved, and he had a large skull tattooed on his right bicep. The tattoo matched the one on the back of his leather vest. "If it makes you feel better, I'll be too busy to enjoy the nice weather too," Brett said, his eyes never leaving the guy.

Perhaps picking up on his distraction, Jen glanced over her shoulder. "Is something wrong?"

"The guy at the counter doesn't fit in here." Everyone else in the bakery was either dressed as if they'd just left work or looked to be college students. The guy at the counter looked like he belonged at a biker bar, not a downtown café.

"Oh, he comes in here a lot." Jen looked back at him. "I think he works in the city because I've seen him at lunchtime wearing a suit."

He couldn't imagine the man in a suit.

"If you don't plan on enjoying your last few days of freedom, what will you be doing?" Jennifer asked, returning to their conversation before he got distracted by the man ordering.

"Getting my campaign up and going."

"You need to start now? The election is more than a year away."

"Slight change in plans. Senator Brown's death means the state will be holding a special election in December."

"I wondered what would happen when I read he'd died. How does a special election work anyway?"

Brett spent the next half hour explaining the process. From there they proceeded to talk about everything from her work to what upcoming movies they were both looking forward to. Talking to her was similar to talking to any of his other friends.

"Yikes, is it really after eight?" Jennifer asked after checking her watch. Like him, she'd just finished her third cup of coffee, although she opted for decaf while he'd stuck with the real stuff.

It seemed like he'd just arrived, but his watch confirmed they'd been talking for almost two hours. "Affirmative."

She slipped her bag's straps onto her shoulder. "I hate to leave, but my dog is going to be starving." She slid out from behind the table. It was the first time since he walked in that she'd stood up. "He probably has his legs crossed too. He hasn't been outside since this morning."

Brett didn't hesitate to stand too. He'd been raised to be a gentleman. However, he was still a man, and he couldn't help but give her a quick once-over. And he liked what he saw. Unlike the actresses so popular in Hollywood, she had a perfect hourglass figure. Even better, she was tall. He stood six two and she was only a few inches shorter than him without any heels.

"We don't want that. I'll walk you to your car."

"You're parked near North Main. My garage is in the opposite direction. Don't worry about it," Jen said.

Even if good manners hadn't been drilled into him all his life, he would've offered to walk with her. He'd enjoyed their time together tonight and wasn't eager for it to come to an end. "It's a nice night, and I need the exercise. Humor me."

Jen shrugged and the strap of her bag slipped from her shoulder. "They're your feet."

He pushed the strap back into place. Her sleeveless blouse left her entire arm bare, and he skimmed his fingers across her skin, amazed at how soft it felt. With the strap no longer a good reason to be touching her, he moved his hand to her lower back. "After you."

Unfortunately, he couldn't think of a good reason to maintain the contact as they walked down Benefit Street and toward a parking garage near her office building.

"This is me." She stopped alongside a dark green Mustang

and used the key fob to unlock the door. He remembered Jen's excitement when she told him she'd finally bought her dream car.

Jen opened the door. "I'm glad we met tonight."

"Me too."

"Good luck on Monday. Let me know how it goes." She tossed her bag in the car but made no movement to get in despite her earlier comment about her dog being starving. Instead her eyes dropped to his lips and then quickly met his again. "And if you're in Providence again let me know. We can meet for coffee or lunch."

He interpreted her statement to mean they were on the same page. "Are you free Saturday?"

"Uh, yeah. Free all weekend. Why?"

"Let's go to the beach and work on your tan." In more than one of her e-mails she'd talked about how much she enjoyed the beach. If the weather was as nice as predicted, they could spend a good portion of the day there.

Actual concern, an odd reaction to his invitation, crossed her face. "The beach," she said rather than answer him.

"We can do something else, but you did mention your tan earlier. And I haven't been to the beach in a while." He didn't date often. When he did ask out a woman, he didn't get turned down. Actually, never in his life had a woman turned him down.

"It is supposed to be a nice day. Okay, sure. A Saturday at the beach sounds nice," she said, sounding uncertain.

He'd sent her enough letters to have her address memorized. "How does 0900...." Brett stopped. "Sorry. Is nine o'clock too early?"

A smile replaced her concerned expression. "I knew what you meant. My dad was in the Army. Nine sounds good. See you then."

Before she could get behind the wheel, he stepped closer. "Have a safe drive home." His eyes zeroed in on her lips. With his target acquired, he leaned toward her. Before he reached his destination, she moved and dropped a quick, sisterly kiss on his cheek.

"Bye." She jumped into her car like a jack-in-the-box going in reverse.

Brett stood and watched her drive away. He hadn't been looking for or expecting it, but a unique relationship had developed thanks to their letters. He wouldn't quite label it as a romantic one yet, but something damn close. He'd asked to meet so he could better gauge what did or didn't exist between them. So far, his preliminary findings pointed in the right direction. This weekend he'd continue gathering intel, a mission he was definitely looking forward to.

CHAPTER 3

JEN LOOKED BACK at her sister. Needing a little moral support this morning, she'd called Kristen. Her sister hadn't hesitated to come over. "What was I thinking?"

Jen tossed another bathing suit on her bed. She didn't wait for Kristen to answer before continuing. "I should've suggested we go for a hike or a bike ride. Maybe a movie. Do you think it's too late to call and reschedule?" Unless you were a fashion model, the beach was a terrible place for a date.

"I'm not letting you reschedule." Kristen picked up the newest suit to land on the bed. "And you can*not* wear this one." She tossed the purple bathing suit back at Jen.

She caught it and then held it up to check for any holes or worn-out spots. She didn't see any. In fact, she didn't see anything wrong with it. The one-piece was her favorite color and the attached skirt covered the scar on her hip nicely. She'd worn it to the beach earlier in the summer. "Why not? I only bought it last year. It looks fine to me."

Before answering, Kristen came over, grabbed it, and stuffed it back into the drawer under the pile of underwear. "Because it's a granny suit." She riffled through the drawer and pulled out the white bikini buried at the bottom. "This is what you should wear." She held the swimsuit up.

Jen eyed the bikini. Her last boyfriend had bought it for a cruise they took together. She'd worn it then to make him happy, but she'd been uncomfortable every time. Now she only wore it if she was lying out alone in her fenced-in backyard and working on her tan. She grabbed the bikini and tossed it back in the drawer where it belonged. "Yeah, no way am I wearing that today." She walked to her bed and grabbed the two tankinis from the pile. "How about one of these?"

"I still think the white one is the way to go, but go with the red one. It's better than all the frumpy one-piece suits you have."

She liked to swim and made a point to visit the gym at least twice a week to get in some laps. Modest one-piece bathing suits were ideal for that. "They're not frumpy. They're practical."

"Whatever you say, as long as you leave them all buried at home today," Kristen said.

Jen stuck her tongue out in her sister's direction before carrying her clothes into the master bathroom. Most of the beaches she visited had changing facilities. Some even had shower stalls. She had no idea where Brett planned to go this morning, so just in case there was no place to change, she'd wear her suit under her clothes. The sundress she'd chosen dried quickly, so if she had to put it over a damp swimsuit later, it wouldn't be a big deal.

"What else are you doing today?" Kristen's voice carried through the closed door.

Excellent question. If Brett had other plans for them, he hadn't shared them with her. She hadn't asked in any of the numerous text messages they'd exchanged since their meeting earlier in the week either. Instead she'd avoided the topic of today's outing altogether, because even thinking about it made the excited knot in her stomach grow exponentially.

"No clue."

Through the door she heard the doorbell ring, followed by Bo's bark. "Shoot, what time is it?" She'd left her watch on the nightstand.

"A few minutes before nine."

Already? She'd known it was getting close, but she thought she had a little more time. "Can you get the door for me?"

"I'm on it."

"Tell him I'll be right down," she said, although she wasn't sure if Kristen heard.

In the past, she'd mentally roll her eyes when she saw women at the beach or pool wearing makeup. This morning she joined their ranks and applied both foundation and lip gloss. Half the fun of visiting the beach was swimming, and she intended on doing some today. Since she'd prefer to not resemble a raccoon at any point during the day, she skipped the mascara and eye shadow.

"Don't ramble today," she said to the reflection in the mirror. "And avoid staring at his lips."

More than once she'd caught herself doing that very thing while he spoke. Considering the man had a gorgeous mouth, it was hard to keep from staring. The final time she'd done it in the parking garage, she'd almost kissed him. She'd stopped herself in the nick of time. Well, more or less stopped. Most would consider the peck on the cheek she'd given him a kiss, but at least it wasn't the type of kiss she'd given him later in her dream. Kissing wasn't all they'd done in her dream either. She couldn't remember ever having such an erotic dream in her life. Just thinking about it now made her face warm.

She found Kristen and Brett in the living room chatting away like long-lost siblings. No matter the person or situation, Kristen could carry on a conversation with them. Since her sister worked in sales, it came in handy. Despite whatever conversation they were having, Brett stood when she entered the room.

"Sorry, I'm running a little behind this morning," she said.

Unlike when he greeted her Tuesday night, this morning he gave her a brief hug and a brotherly kiss on the cheek, causing her heart to jerk wildly in her chest.

"I'm in no rush. Take your time," he said.

Behind him, Kristen gave her a thumbs-up before petting Bo, who had jumped on the sofa near her.

"I'm all set." She glanced back at her sister. "Bo's leash is in the kitchen." With no idea how late she'd be back, she'd asked Kristen to take the dog for the night.

Considering whom the man called family, she expected an Italian sports car worth more than her house to be in the driveway. Instead, a jet-black Corvette was parked behind her sister's new minivan.

Before she could do it, Brett opened the passenger door. "If you give me your bag, I'll throw it in the trunk with mine."

"This car has a trunk?" Corvettes always caught her eye on the road and in parking lots. Although gorgeous vehicles, she assumed they didn't provide their owners with much empty space.

He nodded and held out his hand. "It's not big, but it'll hold what we need today."

Brett waited until she sat before he closed the door. In the side mirror she watched him walk to the back of the car. Tuesday night he'd worn khakis and a polo-style shirt. She thought he'd looked good then. Somehow today, dressed in cargo shorts that hugged his ass and a plain gray T-shirt, he looked even better. Images from her erotic dream surfaced and heat washed over her.

No, no, no. She squeezed her eyes closed. Carrying on a conversation would be impossible if she kept envisioning the man naked and making love to her.

Warmer air filled the car, and she opened her eyes as Brett got behind the wheel.

"Did that tree come down during the storm last weekend?" Brett turned the key and the powerful car roared to life.

Jen looked in the direction of where her new shed had been. Now the tall oak tree, which had come down during the storm with enough force to rip the roots from the ground, was on top of it.

"Yeah, but better my shed than the garage or house. I have a tree company coming this week to take care of it." If the tree had landed on her garage, it would've damaged her new Mustang. She'd lusted after one for years, and after getting her promotion, she'd traded in her Mazda and bought one. She hated the monthly car payments but loved the car.

Brett shifted into reverse and backed into the street. "You should've told me. I would've brought my chainsaw today and taken care of it for you."

She watched him shift into first gear, and itched to ask him for a chance to drive. Unlike a lot of people, she drove a standard. Dad had made sure he taught all his children how, and although her previous car had been an automatic, when she bought her new one, she'd made sure to get a standard. While shifting during rush traffic was a pain, she found driving a standard to be a lot more fun, especially on deserted side roads. And she knew driving this car would be an absolute blast.

She tore her eyes away from his hand as images from the recent dream he'd starred in resurfaced. "You own a chainsaw?" Dad owned every power tool imaginable, including a drill press, and even he didn't own a chainsaw.

He nodded. "I didn't lose any trees but a lot of large limbs came down during the storm. I bought one to take care of them. Spent a few hours Thursday cutting them up. I found it oddly satisfying, and now I've got some firewood for the winter."

"Next time I'm in the need of tree work, I'll call you."

~

He didn't own a home in Newport. As much as he loved the beach and the area, he saw no reason to purchase one anytime soon either, because many of his relatives already had houses there. Since they did, today he planned to take advantage of it. After his meeting with Carl Filmore, his new campaign manager, earlier this week, he'd driven to his brother's house and picked up the key to Curt's beach house. While Newport had more than its share of beautiful public beaches, Curt's place had access to a private beach. His brother's house also offered them many amenities a public beach wouldn't, such as a fully stocked kitchen and a gas grill.

Brett passed the Tennis Hall of Fame and turned left. He'd visited the gated community were both his brother and his cousin's houses were a handful of times. While it could be reached a few different ways, from what he remembered, this was the most direct route, even if it did mean driving through the heart of the city.

From the passenger seat, Jen finished telling him about the camping trip she'd gone on with her Girl Scout troop in July. So far on the ride down they'd covered a wide range of topics, including work, his new house, and her niece's recent birthday party. Not once during the drive had they lapsed into an awkward silence, and Jen never dominated the conversation. More often than he'd care to admit, both situations arose when he took the time to date. It was just one of the reasons he didn't do it often.

He shifted into first gear and turned right. Reaching the security gate, he punched in the code Curt had given him and waited for the gates to open, causing Jen to stop speaking midsentence.

"Did you decide to skip the beach today?" she asked.

"Nope." He drove through the entrance and down the tree-lined street. The community consisted of six homes. Curt's was the last one on the street.

"Maybe beaches look different in Virginia, but this looks like a private neighborhood, not a beach area."

He passed by his cousin's place. Derek and his wife spent most of their time at their house here, but they still owned an apartment in Providence as well. He'd called him yesterday but had only gotten Derek's voice mail. "We're going to my brother's house. This community has access to its own private beach."

Brett reached the last house and pulled into the driveway. "By coming here, we have some privacy and the use of my brother's kitchen." Unable to open the garage door from his car, he parked in the driveway. "Unless you object, I planned to grill us lunch. Later we can maybe go to the Red Parrot for a drink."

"Or Pirate's Cove for ice cream," Jen said.

He couldn't remember the last time he'd visited Pirate's Cove. Whenever he'd come to Newport in the summer as a kid, he'd visited the popular ice cream and mini golf facility with his brother and sister and cousins. He didn't think he'd been there since high school.

"I haven't thought of that place in years." Brett opened his car door and walked around to the passenger side. When he got there, she'd already opened her door.

He held out his hand anyway. She hesitated for a second but then accepted it. "We went last summer when we brought Bella down to see the Tall Ships. It was the first time I've been in a few years. Personally, I think they have the best ice cream. I wish they sold it in stores," Jen said. "Actually, maybe it's better they don't. I'd be eating it all the time."

Brett opened the trunk and pulled out his bag first. Before he could grab Jen's bag, she did it herself and slipped the straps over her shoulder. "I would've gotten it for you." He might not play the role of a perfect gentleman every day, but he knew how it was done. Both Dad and his uncles had made sure of it.

"No need. I got it."

He'd learned though their numerous communications that she was independent and preferred to do things for herself. Rather than risk annoying her this morning, he let the matter go and closed the trunk.

"Whatever you want to do while we're down here is fine with me," Brett said.

The inside of the house looked unchanged from his last visit, with one exception: the brown teddy bear lying on one of the blue-and-white-striped chairs. During their visit, Curt mentioned he'd brought his girlfriend and what turned out to be her niece down recently. He wasn't a relationship guru, but after watching his younger brother interact with his girlfriend both at their cousin's house and then again this week, he expected Curt to be making a trip to the altar soon. When he did, it would leave his cousin Alec and him as the only two unmarried Sherbrooke men. He didn't know how, but most of the females in the family had somehow avoided it so far. Of the six Sherbrooke women, only two were married.

"There's a bathroom off the hall." Brett pulled open the blinds covering the glass doors. "The kitchen is through there." He pointed over his shoulder before sliding the doors open and allowing in fresh ocean air.

"Now this is a view." Rather than head for the bathroom, she came to stand alongside him. "Why doesn't your brother live here all the time?"

As he watched the waves roll onto the beach, he wondered the same thing. "Because he's an idiot."

Jen nudged him in the side, the first contact she'd instigated so far today. "You've talked about your brother enough, so I know you don't mean that."

She spoke the truth. In the beginning, he hadn't spoken much about his family. All too often people couldn't look past his last name and who resided on his family tree. Eventually, it'd been natural to share such details though. And she'd shared plenty of personal information as well, even sometimes telling him about the men she dated. Although as far as he knew, she hadn't been with anyone in a long time—at least, she hadn't mentioned going out with anyone in roughly ten months.

"Curt likes renovating old homes. This spring he bought one up in New Hampshire. It's maybe ten or fifteen minutes over the Massachusetts border." Curt had finished up a few homes before, and each time he'd sold them afterward and moved on. Brett knew his brother wouldn't be selling this one. "His girlfriend lives next door, so it's more convenient for him to live up there than here."

"Proximity does make relationships easier," Jen said.

"Wouldn't know, but I'll take your word for it." His longest relationship ever had lasted six months while he'd been stationed in Texas. It'd ended long before he'd been deployed.

"I don't know about you, but I'm ready to feel some sand between my toes. And I already have my bathing suit on."

"Feel free to head down. I'll be right out."

Brett found her on a beach towel large enough for two full-grown men to use at once. He paused in his approach and watched her apply sunscreen to her right leg. She started at her ankle and moved her hands up, similar to the way he'd touched her in his dream. In his dream though, he hadn't used hands. Instead he'd used his lips and tongue, moving up over her thigh and not stopping until he reached between her legs. Then he'd proceeded to pleasure her until she called out his name. He'd woken up hard and extremely uncomfortable Tuesday night. The dream had made a repeat performance last night.

He dropped the cooler he'd brought down before taking a seat. His eyes roamed across her bare legs. "Need any help?" He wasn't above applying sunscreen if it meant getting his hands on her naked skin.

"Can you get my back?" She looked at him, but the sunglasses she'd slipped on hid her eyes from him. He understood why she'd put them on, but he'd prefer to see her eyes. Eyes told you a lot about what a person was thinking and feeling. With hers covered, he found himself at a disadvantage.

She held the sunscreen toward him. "I'll return the favor," she said.

Jen's bathing suit top tied around her neck, leaving much of her back and shoulders bare. A dusting of freckles covered her shoulders, and he wondered if she had some anywhere else. The modest swimsuit covered more than it revealed, a definite downside as far as he was concerned.

His hands glided over silky skin, and he took his time covering her shoulders. Before she became suspicious or complained he was taking too long, he moved his attention to her back and then lower across her spine.

She sighed before turning around to look at him. Brett's gazed focused on her lips. "Your turn." She moved into a kneeling position and waited for him to turn.

In the parking garage, she'd moved before he could kiss her. With her lips locked in his sights again, he intended to reach his target this time.

He grazed her lips with his and planted his hands on either side of her waist. He kept the kiss undemanding until he felt her relax beneath his palms. Leaning into him, Jen slipped her arms over his shoulders. Changing the angle of his head, he moved his mouth over hers, devouring its softness. Before he could do it, she urged his lips apart and dipped her tongue inside his mouth, sending a wave of lust and desire through his body.

In his head, he ran through the best ways to get them both horizontal. The sudden bump to the head stopped him from executing any of them.

"What the...?" He pulled away and found a football near his

feet. Glancing up, he scanned the area as a teenage girl jogged toward them. They'd had the beach to themselves when he came outside. The teen headed their way said the situation had changed.

"Sorry," the girl said nervously when she reached them. "My stupid brother threw it over my head." She pointed over her shoulder.

Brett looked past the girl toward the house next door. Another teenager, perhaps two or three years older than the girl, stood on the beach with a smirk on his face. Three others remained on the deck. Accidents happened, but the teenager's expression said this hadn't been an accident. He'd aimed for Brett's head.

"Don't worry about it." Picking up the ball, he tossed it back to the girl. "Tell your brother to be more careful."

"I will," she promised before jogging away.

With others on the beach, any thoughts he had of taking things further went on hold. Later he'd probably be happy about that. The occasional one-night stand was fine, but he was ready for more in his life. Now that he was living in New England again, he intended to see if he could have it with Jen, because at some point in the past year, his feelings for her had changed from mere friendship to something else. Her response to his kiss suggested the same on her end.

"Are you okay?" she asked.

"Fine for the moment. But if you don't get some sunscreen on my back soon, we'll have a problem." With a bunch of teenagers hanging around next door, they needed to keep their hands and lips to themselves as long as they were outside. Applying sunscreen to his body would give them an acceptable excuse to touch. He'd take what he could get for the immediate future.

THE GUY COULD GRILL. No matter how many times she tried, she couldn't cook anything on a grill. It always came out one of two ways: burned past recognition, or black on the outside but raw on the inside. Despite having a practically brand-new gas grill in her backyard, she hadn't cooked on it once all summer. Instead, either Dad or her brother-in-law used it when they came over for a cookout. In return, she handled all the sides and desserts. She might not be able to grill, but she loved baking. And she was darn good at it, if she did say so herself.

He's an even better kisser. Jen watched him through the glass doors. She'd laughed when Kristen said Dan didn't merely kiss her, but made love to her mouth. After this morning, she knew what her sister meant. She'd felt Brett's kiss everywhere. If not for the teens on the beach with them, she would've tried for another. Unfortunately, the teens who had interrupted them hours ago had remained on the beach until after Brett finished grilling their steaks. And while the group was gone now, it was anyone's guess when they or any other residents might return to enjoy the beach.

The glass door slid open, and Brett stepped out on the deck. Before he started cooking, he'd thrown on a T-shirt, much to her disapproval. Unfortunately, he still wore it now.

"Sorry about that." He dropped into the padded deck chair next to her.

She'd had time to enjoy a gorgeous view and the sunshine. She had nothing to complain about. "Don't worry about it. Is everything okay?"

"Yeah, it was Carl."

She knew all his relatives' names, or at least she thought she did. Carl didn't sound familiar. "Carl? Another cousin?"

Brett reached across the space separating them and tucked the loose strand of hair dancing against her cheek behind her ear. "No. I thought I told you. I hired Carl Filmore to run my

43

campaign. He called to let me know we have about half the signatures necessary to get me on the ballot for the upcoming primary."

She didn't know the exact number of signatures required. Considering they were talking about the United States Senate and not a state-level position, she guessed it was a lot. "Already?"

"Name recognition has its perks. Having an uncle who is also a popular president in the White House helps too."

It was the first time he'd made any comment about how influential and well known his family was. "When we started exchanging letters, I assumed it was a coincidence your name was Brett Sherbrooke."

"Really?" He sounded surprised by her admission.

She shrugged. "It's not uncommon for people to share a name with someone famous. I had a classmate at Northeastern named Anderson Brady, and he was definitely not the actor." She had been mildly disappointed when she finally met the man and learned he wasn't the actor but rather a middle-aged man from Cambridge, Massachusetts.

"Yeah, but your brother knew who I was. Keith never said anything?"

"Nope. At least not to Kristen or me. I didn't figure it out until you mentioned your cousin Trent's wedding. I could accept you shared a name with someone in *the* Sherbrooke family. But having a cousin named Trent was too much of a coincidence."

Brett frowned. Somehow even frowning he looked handsome. "Most people figure it out a lot sooner. It's the one thing I'm not looking forward to now that I'm not on active duty."

She'd spotted enough pictures of his cousins on various websites and magazine covers to know how much the media loved his family. People invading your privacy had to be annoying.

"Well, if you need a good bodyguard, I'm available," she

said, hoping to change his frown back into a smile. "My hand-to-hand combat skills are not quite as good as my forensic accounting skills, but I can hold my own in a fight. Dad and Keith made sure I could take care of myself."

Her statement did the trick, and his frown vanished. "Having you around twenty-four seven is a tempting offer. But I'd rather have your attention on me, not on whatever media vulture might be lurking around." He leaned across the space between them, his intent obvious.

When his lips touched hers, a shock wave went through her body. Closing her eyes, she lost herself in the kiss and the heat building up inside her. Who he was didn't matter, only the fact she was here with him, and he seemed as interested in her as she was in him did. Parting her lips, she ran her tongue along his bottom lip, a silent message to open. He didn't hesitate, and she immediately took control of their kiss. At least until Brett moved and his lips seared a path down her neck to her bare shoulder.

She sensed his hand going for the tie behind her neck. While her body said "go for it," her mind screamed "put on the brakes." Reaching up, she covered his hand with hers. Whether he'd intended to stop or not before she touched his hand, he placed a final kiss on her shoulder before touching his forehead to hers.

"It kills me to say this," she said, a little out of breath. "Maybe we should go someplace public for a little while." A place with a lot of people would keep her from tugging him to the nearest bed and having her way with the man.

Brett pulled back and kissed her forehead. "I could go for some ice cream."

～

LOCATED ON WELLINGTON AVENUE, Pirate's Cove was a popular destination for both tourists and locals. When he'd come as a kid, it had comprised of only the large eighteenth-century stone building before them and a small mini golf course. The complex in front of them now was something else entirely. While the stone building with the flashing neon Open sign remained, the tiny mini golf course was long gone. Now to the left of the building sat an enormous eighteen-hole mini golf course complete with a windmill and waterfall. From where they stood, he saw at least six batting cages behind the building, and off to the far right was a go-cart track.

"This place has changed," Brett said. "I used to come here all the time, and it looked nothing like this." He reached the door handle before Jen and pulled it open for her.

"Did you spend a lot of time down here when you were younger?"

They stepped inside and the smell of fresh-made waffle cones and hot fudge wafted around him. The scent conjured up long forgotten memories of walking over with his brother and cousins. "At least two weeks every summer, but usually more. We'd stay at Cliff House. At least all the kids would. The adults took turns supervising us. Aunt Elizabeth was always the strictest of the bunch. I love her, but we always had more fun when she wasn't around. We never got away with anything when she was there. Aunt Marilyn, on the other hand, was a pushover."

A memory he hadn't thought of in a long time involving his Aunt Elizabeth popped up, and he laughed. It wasn't the first time this week a long-forgotten memory involving his family surfaced. Each time one did, he realized how much he'd missed them the past few years. Sure he'd seen them from time to time, but he hadn't been a real part of their lives. Instead he'd been like the distant relative who visited for family reunions and weddings.

"What's so funny?" Jen asked.

"Thinking about one of the nights my brother refused to eat

dinner. Aunt Elizabeth wouldn't let him leave the table until he tried everything on his plate. Curt fell asleep sitting there and landed face-first in his food. I don't think Curt ever refused again after that."

"My mom had a similar rule. Thankfully, I usually liked what she cooked. My sister was always the picky one. My brother would eat anything not moving." Jen joined the line at the counter. "So, what flavor are you going to order? Last time I came here, I had the banana bread. It was out of this world. My niece had the cherry explosion. She insisted I try some. I don't usually love cherries, but it was good too."

The board on the wall listed easily fifty different ice-cream flavors in addition to the ones Jen mentioned and several types of frozen yogurt. He didn't need to read any of them. "Vanilla in a waffle cone." When he got ice cream, he always ordered vanilla.

"Vanilla? Are you serious? That's like the most boring flavor in the world," Jen said.

"Boring is my cousin's middle name," a familiar voice said from behind them.

They both turned and faced the newest additions to the line, his cousin Derek and his wife, Brooklyn.

"It's better than your middle name." He ignored Derek for the moment and hugged Brooklyn instead. When he finished he said, "Jen, this is Brooklyn, my cousin's wife." It felt natural to put his arm around Jen as the two women exchanged greetings.

"If vanilla is so boring, what are you getting?" Brett asked without another glance in his cousin's direction.

Derek responded more or less the way he expected. "I stand corrected. His middle names are boring and rude." His cousin extended his hand toward Jen. "Derek, Brett's polite and much more charming cousin."

Jen's mouth twisted as if she was trying not to either laugh or perhaps smile. "I don't know, he's pretty polite and charming when we're together."

Brooklyn nodded. "He's always polite to me too. Derek, the problem must be you."

The friendly banter continued as they waited to order and even after they found a covered picnic table outside to share. Growing up, he'd always given his cousins and siblings a hard time. And they'd always reciprocated. Until this afternoon, he hadn't realized how much he'd missed it.

"I heard an ugly rumor. Something about you running for Senator Neil Brown's seat in the upcoming special election," Derek said, touching on a serious topic.

Great. Another person who found it hard to believe he might want to serve his country in a different way. He'd gotten a similar statement from his sister when he called her earlier in the week too. "If all goes as planned, I'll be on the ballot. I hired Carl Filmore to run things for me. So far, so good."

"You in DC?" Derek dropped his spoon in the ice-cream bowl. "I can't see it. My brother, yeah, or even Sara. But not you."

"Don't listen to him." Brooklyn glared at his cousin as she spoke. "I think you'd make a great senator. We need new faces and ideas on the Hill. If I can help, call me."

"Filmore, huh? He knows what he's doing. He worked on Beck's campaign last year, and he helped with Uncle Warren's first presidential campaign. Dad speculated he'd work on the upcoming one too."

Brett hadn't known either of those details. However, the information reinforced he'd made a good choice. Next to him, Jen shifted nervously. She hadn't said much since they sat down. He'd thought it was because she was eating her ice cream, something called cookie crunch. He wasn't sure what was in it, but it didn't appear to be a flavor he'd enjoy. Glancing at her bowl now, he saw she hadn't touched much of it. Evidently food had nothing to do with her silence. Perhaps a change in conversation was needed.

"Derek and Brooklyn work in Providence too," he said. He looked at his cousin. "Jen works at Pattersen Financial."

Derek took the cue to change subjects. "You're just a few buildings down from us. We're both at Hale and Associates."

CHAPTER 4

JEN ACCEPTED the wine Brooklyn handed her. After finishing their ice cream, they'd played a round of mini golf together. Although a friendly game, Brett and Derek had become ridiculously competitive to the point Brooklyn threatened to leave if they didn't chill out. Jen hadn't minded though. She much preferred the friendly insults they tossed at each other to the political talk they'd exchanged while seated. Hearing them discuss President Sherbrooke and Senator Beck's names the way they had reminded her too well who sat next to her. Thankfully, the conversation had been fairly short-lived. The subject of politics hadn't come up again.

After the game, Derek and his wife invited them back to their house. Now they were all outside enjoying the deck and empty beach. According to Brooklyn, their neighbors hadn't been down all summer. Why someone would purchase a home in such a beautiful location and not use it escaped her. If she had a beach house, she'd be there every chance she got.

Taking a sip of her drink, she listened to the waves crashing on the shore. She wasn't a wine expert, but the wine in her glass was delicious. Across the table, Brooklyn glanced at her again.

She'd done it several times during their time together. This time she snapped her fingers and leaned forward in her chair.

"I knew I'd seen you before," she said. "You do the lead vocals for Black Velvet." Brooklyn didn't wait for Jen to confirm or deny the statement. Instead she touched her husband's arm and continued. "Derek, we've seen her perform at the Red Parrot."

She'd been performing with the local band for over three years and rarely did anyone recognize her. Jen was surprised Brooklyn did tonight.

"I thought you looked familiar," Derek said. "When and where is the band's next performance?"

"You perform?" Brett asked, looking at her.

She took another sip of her wine. She'd love to get this kind for her house, assuming the price tag wasn't ridiculous. "I told you I did." It wasn't a secret she tried to hide from people. Even her niece knew she performed with a band. In fact, Bella kept asking when she'd be old enough to come and watch a show.

"You mentioned you sang. But never said anything about performing with a band. I would've remembered."

Brett seemed to remember everything else she'd told him. If this news was a surprise to him, then she must've never mentioned it. "It's not a big deal. We used to perform about twice a month or so. Things have been off since the spring. Jim, our drummer, and his wife had a baby in March. And about two weeks later, I got my promotion." She thought back over the past few months. "Last time we performed was in May. We were at a club in Warwick."

"Next time you have a performance, let us know. We'd love to come and see you. You've got an incredible voice," Brooklyn said.

She'd never been comfortable accepting compliments. Tonight was no different and heat filled her face. She didn't need a mirror to know she'd turned a nice shade of her least favorite

color, pink. "Thanks. Singing is something I've done forever."
Even in high school she'd sung in the chorus.

Jen took the final sip of wine, and before she could stop
herself, she yawned. She had no idea of the time. She'd left her
watch at home and hadn't taken her cell phone from her bag all
day. Stars and an almost full moon filled the sky though, so it
had to be on the later side.

Across the table, Brooklyn yawned too. "Sorry. I'm
exhausted all of a sudden," she said.

"Honestly, I'm starting to fade too," Derek said. "You're
welcome to spend the night. We've got the room. And tomorrow
Brooklyn and I plan to take the *Affinity* over to Martha's Vineyard. Join us. It'll give me a chance to fill Jen in on all your
embarrassing childhood moments."

"Thanks, but I've got a meeting with Filmore tomorrow."
Brett pushed his chair away from the table. "Maybe another
weekend, assuming Jen can handle being in your company
again." He extended his hand toward her. "What do you think?
Could you stomach my cousin's company for another several
hours?"

Thanks to the lights on the deck, she spotted the humor in his
eyes. She'd thought her brother Keith enjoyed giving family
members a hard time, but Brett enjoyed it even more.

She took her time before answering, as if she really needed
to consider the question. In reality though, there was no need.
She'd had a delightful time with Derek and Brooklyn and would
happily do it again. "Yes, I think I could tolerate it. But not
too often."

Brett laughed and kissed her cheek. "I knew we got along
well for a reason."

After a quick stop at his brother's house to pick up their
things and one at a downtown coffee shop, they got on the
highway. She didn't know about him, but she needed the
caffeine pick-me-up. Without it she might fall asleep on the

ride home. She'd rather not snore during their first formal date.

"You seem close to your cousin Derek. Are you like that with the rest of your family?" Jen asked as they crossed over the Newport Bridge.

He'd spoken fondly of his family in his letters, and she'd read in numerous places the Sherbrookes were a tight-knit group. Until this evening, she hadn't realized just how close. And she was a tad jealous. While she was close to her parents and Kristen and Keith, she didn't have a large extended family like Brett.

"Affirmative. We're all around the same age." He glanced at her briefly. "Some of my cousins have tighter relationships with each other than others. Jake and Trent are the closest, I think. Only a few months separate them in age, and they did everything together until college. They even had kids within months of each other."

She heard disappointment or something close to it in his voice but didn't comment. Whatever emotions he was experiencing were his business. If he wanted to share them with her, he would. "You're lucky. I always wanted a big family like yours."

She might want a large extended family similar to Brett's, but she'd never complain about what she had either, considering what her life had been like before Reggie and Erica Wallace adopted her. A time she remembered quite well.

The garage floodlight went on, and she watched Brett shift the car into neutral. Hours ago she'd been thinking about canceling their day at the beach. Back to where their day had started, she was so happy she hadn't acted on the impulse.

"My meeting with Filmore tomorrow starts at noon. I don't know how long I'll be," Brett said. He turned off the car then shifted his position so he faced her. "If it's like our first meeting, it'll be a while."

She followed politics enough to make an educated decision

at the polls. Outside of that, she knew next to nothing about what went into a campaign. "I hope the meeting is more interesting than our quarterly staff meetings. Those are boring enough to put even an insomniac to sleep."

She dreaded the quarterly staff meetings the office insisted on holding. As far as she knew, everyone in the office did, including the accounting firm's president. Still, every quarter another one popped up on the calendar.

"Doubt it." He reached over and took her hand. "We're meeting at his office in Boston. If it's not too late, do you want to meet for dinner?" The pad of his thumb rubbed against her palm, sending tiny sparks of heat up her arm.

She'd agreed to work on plans for their upcoming Girl Scout meetings tomorrow. Kristen would understand if she rescheduled. Actually, she'd probably encourage it. For at least the past year, her sister had been urging her to date more. She'd even tried to set Jen up with some of Dan's friends. Each time, Jen had come up with some excuse to not go. However, the real reason was currently sitting across from her. Back then she'd kept her mouth closed about it. She'd been too afraid if she told Kristen she didn't want to date other men because she was half in love with a guy she'd never met, her sister would think she'd lost her sanity. After all, it was a silly reason, especially since at the time Jen didn't think she'd ever meet Brett. Today proved it hadn't been as ridiculous as she'd once thought.

"Definitely. If it's easier, I can meet you in Boston." She didn't need much of an excuse to drive her new car. But in this case, it also seemed fair. Jen didn't know exactly how far away North Salem was, but he'd driven down twice now to see her. It seemed only right she reciprocate and make the trip north.

He smiled, once again pulling her eyes toward his all-too-perfect mouth. They hadn't kissed since before leaving for Pirate's Cove. This moment seemed like the perfect opportunity to rectify that, and she wasn't willing to wait for him to do it.

Jen leaned toward him and touched her lips to his. Earlier in the afternoon, he let her set the pace of their kiss. Not this time. Instead Brett moved his mouth over hers, his lips communicating both strength and passion. With each second, her heart seemed to thump harder and faster. When he finally pulled away, she searched her mind for a good reason not to invite him inside for the night. Only one popped up.

You're a responsible adult, she reminded herself. Only a crazy teenager would invite Brett over for a slumber party after getting together only twice. Right?

"If tomorrow doesn't end up working out, what does the rest of your week look like?" Brett asked.

Although he'd ended their kiss, his face remained only inches away from hers.

Week? She tried to picture her schedule, not an easy feat with Brett's fingers moving up and down the back of her neck.

"Pretty typical." At least she thought so. Honestly, she wasn't completely certain because she couldn't focus on anything but his skin on hers.

"MONDAY AND TUESDAY are out for me," Brett said.

"I have plans for Wednesday already." She sounded as disappointed as he felt.

He probably shouldn't make any plans until after his meeting with Filmore and the rest of his campaign team tomorrow. He remembered the first time his uncle ran for the US Senate. The campaign had taken over his life. If he wanted to win first the primary and then the election, he should devote all his time and energy to the campaign and nothing else. In that respect, starting anything with Jen was a bad idea. Bad idea or not, he planned on carrying it out. If he couldn't see her tomorrow, he didn't want to wait until next weekend, but he didn't think he had much of a choice.

"How's Friday after work?"

"All yours," she said.

"Outstanding." He opened his car door. "I'll grab your stuff."

Like she had at his brother's house, she didn't wait for him to come around and open her door. Instead she met him at the back of the car. This time though he pulled her bag out before she could. After closing the trunk, he took her hand.

The lights flanking the front door switched on when they approached the steps, and he wondered if she'd invite him inside. It was well past midnight already, and he had roughly an hour and a half drive home. If she asked him to stay, he should say no. He wouldn't.

He waited for her to unlock the door. "I'll call you as soon as my meeting ends."

"Great." She accepted the bag he held toward her. "Be careful driving home. I can make you a coffee to take with you if you think you need it."

It'd been a long time since someone sounded so concerned about his well-being. His family worried about him, but they never voiced it anymore. Not even Mom. "Don't worry about it. If I need something, I'll stop on my way."

ACCORDING to the background Dad provided, Carl Filmore had worked on his first political campaign while still in college. It had been for a small local race in the western part of the state. Since then Carl had devoted his life to one thing: getting his candidate elected regardless of the office he or she was running for. More times than not, Carl succeeded.

"Do you believe Brett's lack of political experience will be an issue?" Dad asked. Although his presence wasn't necessary, Brett had asked Dad to join them today. Dad hadn't hesitated to agree. He'd even canceled his golf game with Brett's uncle Mark so he could come, and Jonathan Sherbrooke never canceled a golf game.

"We've seen several candidates with no tested political experience over the past few years win," Carl said once his personal assistant again left the room. The woman had made several trips in and out of the office since Brett sat down. "Many of us believe it's society's way of saying they're tired of old Washington. Last year two unknowns with zero experience defeated incumbents for seats in Congress. And according to the polls, the race between Senator Eason and Tara Wakefield in Arizona is a tight one. Wakefield held only a town-level office before entering the race. I really think the race out there could go either way in November."

Dad added milk and sugar to his coffee. "I've been following the race in Arizona and was shocked when I saw the polls this week."

"And it's not like we have any negative baggage to worry about in addition to no political experience." Carl looked in his direction. "Brett, you've got a flawless reputation. The kind men like me dream our candidates will have going into an election. Combine it with your military record and your last name, and this campaign could practically run itself."

Brett didn't want to win solely based on his family name. He'd spent most of his life making sure he achieved his goals on his own, not because he'd been born into the right family. However, if this one time his last name helped him get where he wanted to be so he could make a real difference in government, he'd use it.

"Unless either of you has any more questions about what we've discussed so far, let's move to the next item on the agenda," Carl said.

"Only one," Dad said. "How are we doing with the nomination papers?"

"Going on schedule," Brett answered before Carl spoke.

Before Dad arrived, they'd reviewed Carl's expected timetable for collecting the rest of the signatures required. Brett was pleased he expected the nomination papers to be ready for submission before the end of the week.

"Let's move on to item number two," Brett said. After years of giving orders, he found it difficult to leave even the running of this meeting to someone else.

Carl checked his agenda and nodded. "I know Lily has already contacted Pam Burton at the *Boston Times*. She wants to do a sit-down interview with you next week," he said, referring to Lily Pierce, Brett's campaign press secretary. She was the only key member of Brett's inner team not present for today's meeting. "She's got a call in to the *Worcester Daily News* as well."

He'd read countless interviews his uncles and cousins had given, but he'd never had to do one himself. His lack of experience with the media didn't matter; he still knew how easily reporters could take what you said and twist it. He'd need to be extra vigilant during any interviews he gave.

"We'll also need to get some commercials in the works," Carl continued. "Pedro Jones is my go-to in this area."

Brett intended to have a say in all aspects of his campaign. As far as who to hire for television commercials though, he'd leave that to Carl and his creative team. They'd done this before, he hadn't. "Get him on board. I'm ready when he is."

During their first meeting, they'd discussed his platform for the campaign. He saw no reason to rehash it now. However, he was curious as to who his competition might be. Carl had tossed out a few names earlier in the week, but Brett hadn't seen or read any definite answers yet. If anyone would know though, it'd be Carl. When it came to politics, he had eyes and ears everywhere.

"Any word yet on whom I'll likely be up against?"

"Ted Smith hired Phillip Young to run his campaign. Ted

will be your biggest competition for the party nomination," Carl answered.

He recognized the former lieutenant governor's name. Ted had the political experience, but he also had a severely tarnished reputation thanks to an extramarital scandal followed by a messy divorce five or six years ago. The name Phillip Young sounded familiar too, but he couldn't say why. If he thought of it, he'd ask his dad or one of his cousins if they recognized the name.

"It looks like Gina Hammond and Vince Reed will be the front-runners for their party's nomination. I think in terms of agenda, Gina's the last thing we need in Washington. Many people even in her party agree with me. However, I think Gina's still got an edge over Vince. She has Kevin McGinnis running things. The man will stop at nothing to win."

Brett was vaguely familiar with both names. Gina Hammond had served one term as a representative from Vermont in Congress and then run for Senate. She'd lost to the incumbent, one of Dad's college buddies. If she planned to run in the special election, she'd moved south, perhaps hoping new voters would mean a different outcome. Vince Reed was a professional football player who'd retired after ten seasons with the New England Rebels. Since then he'd earned a law degree and branched out into business. Brett didn't know anything about his political leanings. He'd have to spend some time researching all three potential opponents.

"Interviews and commercials help, but they don't win campaigns. We need to get you out there. Even today a handshake goes a long way to getting a vote. People go with the candidate they feel most connected to. I'll e-mail you the list of events you need to attend. We can discuss more as they come up." Carl looked up from his computer. "Unless you have more questions, let's talk about fund-raising."

He shook his head and turned his attention to the woman across the conference table from him, his finance coordinator.

When Brett walked out of Carl Filmore's office a few hours later, his head was full of talking points, important dates, and dollar signs. He'd gone into the meeting expecting it to be a long one, and he hadn't been disappointed. Despite the lengthy and at times all-out boring afternoon, he felt more confident than before about his chances of winning the primary in November and the special election in December.

"I think today's meeting went well. You made the right decision going with Carl," Dad said as they stepped off the elevator inside the parking garage near Carl's office. "How about we stop for dinner and a drink?" Dad asked. "I'd invite your mom too but she has plans with your aunt Marilyn tonight."

Brett checked his watch. It was around dinnertime. He'd hoped to see Jen again tonight, but he hadn't spent much time with his dad lately. And although they didn't always see eye to eye, he enjoyed spending time with Dad. If he explained to Jen why he couldn't meet her tonight, she'd understand. Family was important to her too.

"Where should we go?" He took out his cell phone and sent Jen a text message.

"I was thinking the clubhouse at Pleasant View."

He'd passed by the entrance to the country club his parents belonged to on his way to today's meeting. As a general rule, he avoided that club as well as the many others Dad and Mom belonged to. He didn't much care for golf. He cared for the majority of society elites who spent their time at the facilities even less. Tonight, he'd make an exception. It wasn't far from where they were, and generally the restaurants at his parents' clubs served excellent food.

"I'll meet you there." The cell phone in his hand beeped, alerting him to a new message.

"Excellent." Dad gave him a slap on the back and walked down the row to his car. Brett watched until Dad got into the vehicle before turning his attention to the device.

Have fun with your dad. See you Friday?

Affirmative. Call you tomorrow.

He'd figure out the logistics for Friday sometime between tonight and their conversation tomorrow.

JEN FLIPPED to the next page in her leader handbook and set her cell phone down. She'd brought all her Girl Scout materials with her when she went to pick up Bo. Bella's impromptu concert had kept them from getting started right away. Her niece had started piano lessons around the New Year, and she regularly liked to perform for anyone who stopped by. Today she'd insisted on playing the newest song she'd mastered, but one song quickly turned into several songs. Eventually a video call from a friend put a halt to the concert, leaving Jen and her sister to start their review of which badges they wanted to tackle this fall.

"I think we should work first on the animal habitats badge," Kristen said without looking up from her handbook. "Or the flowers badge. Both would be easier in the fall. We can do the first aid one in the winter. I know the fire department will help us with it. What do you think?" She looked over at Jen. "Hey, what's up? Bad news?"

She turned to the animal habitats badge before answering. "No, not really. Brett and I talked about getting together after his meeting today. He just texted to say he's going to dinner with his dad instead." They hadn't made definite plans for the night, so she shouldn't be disappointed, but she was.

"A meeting on a Sunday?" Kristen asked.

Her sister had less interest in politics than she did. Every election, Kristen voted for the same candidates and issues as her husband. Still, the death of Senator Neil Brown had been on every news outlet in the country. When Governor Wentworth announced the date of the special election, it had attracted national attention too. With the longtime senator gone, the party's majority in the Senate was in jeopardy. It had already lost the majority in the House of Representatives two years ago. With so much chatter going on, Jen didn't think there was any chance her sister hadn't heard of the upcoming election.

"You heard about the special election being held in Massachusetts to fill Senator Brown's seat, right?"

"Kind of hard not to. It's everywhere. You'd think the election was taking place here, because it even made the front page of the *Providence Gazette*."

She couldn't recall the last time she'd bought a newspaper. Mom and Dad still did though, and Kristen stopped by their house every weeknight to pick up Bella, who stayed with them after school. "Brett's running. He had another meeting with his campaign manager today."

"Makes sense considering his family." Kristen put a bookmark in her handbook and closed it.

Bella's concert had kept them from discussing Jen's date. Once her niece finished up, Jen insisted they get right to work in case Brett called and asked her to meet him. With that possibility off the table, there was no reason not to answer any questions her sister might have.

"If you were talking about seeing each other tonight, yesterday must have gone well," Kristen said. "I got a little worried when you didn't say anything, but didn't want to ask."

More than well as far as she was concerned. "You were right to not let me cancel. Thanks."

"Wait, did I really hear you say that? Maybe you need to repeat yourself."

She could play this game too. "Thanks."

"No, no. The first part, about me being right." Her sister smiled. "C'mon, let me hear you say it."

"*This time* you were right." She couldn't help but put some emphasis on the "this time" part of her statement.

"Details, details. Don't leave me hanging. Where did you go, and what did you do?"

"The beach."

"Well, yes I knew you were going there. What beach? And what did you do after?"

Jen didn't know if the beach they'd spent the day on had a name. "Brett's brother owns a house in Newport. It has access to a private beach. We went there."

"Access to a private beach, sounds nice. His brother wasn't there though, was he?"

"No. Curt lives somewhere in New Hampshire. He let Brett use the house for the day."

Kristen pushed back her chair. "Hold any further details. I need a drink. Want one?" She moved to the refrigerator and pulled out a pitcher of homemade lemonade.

"Some of that would be great." Jen's stomach growled. In a rush to get there this morning, she'd opted for only a protein shake. Bella's performance had taken them straight through lunchtime. "Mind if I grab a snack?"

At the counter, her sister filled two glasses. "Help yourself. You know you don't need to ask."

Jen tossed a bag of popcorn in the microwave. It was her brother-in-law's favorite snack, and Kristen always had plenty on hand.

"Okay, so you went to a private beach. What else? Did he take you to one of the fancy Newport restaurants?" Kristen asked. "I've been dying to visit the Spiced Pear. It's supposed to be incredible. I've been hinting to Dan that I'd like to go there for our anniversary in September."

Jen liked her brother-in-law a lot, but he didn't always pick up on subtle hints. If she were Kristen, she'd flat-out tell Dan she wanted to go to the Spiced Pear or simply make the reservation herself. Otherwise there was a very good chance Dan would come up with something else for their anniversary. "If you guys go down to Newport for your anniversary weekend, Bella can stay with me."

It wasn't uncommon for Bella to spend a weekend with her if Kristen and Dan went away.

"Thanks. I don't know what we're doing yet." Kristen took a long sip of her lemonade. "Back to your date though. Did he take you to dinner?"

The microwave beeped before Jen answered. "Nope." She pulled the bag out and tugged it open. She waited for the steam to escape before filling two bowls. "He grilled us lunch."

"Grilled? Okay, I guess you were at his brother's house so it was probably easy enough. But you did something afterward, right?"

Before she answered, Jen chewed a few pieces of popcorn and then washed it down with her lemonade. "Yep, we went to Pirate's Cove for ice cream and while there we—"

Kristen's glass hit the table with a thud. "You went for ice cream? Seriously, he couldn't come up with anything more, I don't know, elegant? Exciting?"

Just because Kristen didn't think a trip to Pirate's Cove made for a good first date didn't mean there was anything wrong with it. "Actually, going for ice cream was my idea, not his. He suggested going to the Red Parrot." Jen didn't try to hide the annoyance in her voice. "I don't see the big deal."

"It's not a big deal, but you've got to admit it sounds like something two high school kids would do on a first date." Kristen shrugged a shoulder. "I just thought someone with his background would treat you to a more sophisticated first date. Not a grilled lunch at his brother's house and then ice cream."

Her sister's misconception was understandable. What little Kristen and much of the world knew about the Sherbrooke family came from the media. Articles always portrayed them as living the type of lifestyle most people could only dream of experiencing. Perhaps others in Brett's family did live that way.

64

However, it didn't fit the man she'd come to know over the past two years.

"We also played a round of mini golf with Brett's cousin and his cousin's wife. Afterward we went back to their house for a visit." Now, she could picture Derek, Brett's cousin, taking a woman out for a night more in line with what her sister imagined. Although nice and approachable, it was obvious he enjoyed the finer things in life.

Kristen scooped up a handful of popcorn and raised it toward her mouth. "Wow, you're meeting his family members already? Dan and I were engaged before I met most of his family. Which cousin was it? He's got enough of them."

"Derek. He got married last fall." The unexpected wedding had kept the media talking for months. "He has a house in the same neighborhood as Brett's brother. We ran into them when we went for ice cream, so it wasn't planned."

"Well, as long as you had fun it doesn't really matter what you two did."

She'd had fun. She assumed he had too or he wouldn't have asked to see her again. "We did. Now we should probably get back to this." Jen reopened her sister's handbook.

"One last question and we can get back to work," Kristen said.

She'd given her sister a complete breakdown of her day. But if Kristen had one more question, she'd humor her. After all, she'd given Kristen the third degree more than once regarding the men she'd dated before marrying Dan. "Go for it. But only one, I really do want to get this finished so I can go home."

"Since you were at his brother's house, you obviously had access to a bedroom. Did you visit it sometime between lunch and your visit to Pirate's Cove?"

Jen should've expected the question; there wasn't a topic out there either of them considered off-limits. But she hadn't. "No, things didn't go that far yesterday."

"But you kissed at least. Please tell me you did, Jen. The man is gorgeous. He looked even better in person than he did in the pictures."

"We…. Wait a minute. What pictures? I didn't show you the one he sent me." It was safely tucked away in her desk drawer.

Kristen shifted in her seat. "After you told me who you were meeting, I did a search on the internet for a picture. I couldn't help myself."

If the tables had been reversed, Jen might have done the exact same thing. "You shouldn't have done it, but well, I can't say I blame you either."

"I didn't find many, but I think I found the one you did of him with Trent and Jake. He doesn't look anything like his cousins."

She agreed with both her sister's assessments. There was no mistaking Trent and Jake for cousins. They, like many of the other Sherbrookes, greatly resembled each other. She was glad Brett didn't fit the mold. While there was no denying his two cousins were gorgeous men, they were almost a little too handsome.

"I agree the pictures don't do him justice. And to answer what was technically your second question, we kissed." She'd dreamed about those kisses last night too. "Now can we get back to work?"

The sooner they finished, the sooner she could go home and spend some time thinking about the kisses they'd shared.

CHAPTER 5

DESPITE ALL THE growth in nearby towns, North Salem remained on the smaller side and clung to its small town traditions. It was one of the main reasons Brett had picked it last year when he'd decided to buy a home in Massachusetts. At the same time, it was close enough to larger cities for when he found himself in need of a night at a ball game or a concert. After making the drive into Boston and then back home all week, he was reconsidering his decision. He'd tried leaving his house at different times each morning, and it didn't seem to help. The only thing it seemed to change was where he hit the majority of traffic. If he didn't win the election and stayed working for Homeland Security, he might need to get a second place in Boston, because the commute every day would drive him insane. He honestly didn't know how other people did it. Until November though, he'd suck it up and deal. It didn't make any sense to make changes until after he knew whether or not he'd be heading to DC.

Brett took the exit for Salem and checked his watch. *Nineteen*—Brett stopped before he finished the thought. Regardless of where he found himself in six months, he needed to get back in the habit of using civilian time. "Seven o'clock. Damn," he said.

They'd agreed to meet at seven. He'd have to call Jen and let her know he was running behind. He already felt bad enough she'd driven up tonight. He'd tried to change her mind, but she'd refused to budge. She'd insisted it was her turn to make the trip since he'd come down to Rhode Island twice already. Although he'd disagreed, especially since he'd visited his family as well as her during his first trip, he'd stopped trying to change her mind pretty quickly. Her stubbornness rivaled his own, and that was saying a lot.

Brett pressed the phone icon on the car's touch screen. "Call Jen," he said as he turned right and approached a yellow traffic light. The sound of a ringing phone came though the car speakers. After a few rings, Jen's voice replaced it.

"Sorry, I'm still about ten minutes out," he said after greeting her.

"No problem. I just got here. Do you want me to let them know I'm here so we don't lose our table?"

He doubted they'd have a problem getting seated no matter when they arrived. For better or worse, his picture had been plastered on every New England news channel and newspaper this week. One look at him and the restaurant staff would know exactly who he was and what family he belonged to. He didn't share his thoughts. Despite knowing who he was, Jen treated him like any other man, something his week had been lacking so far. He didn't want to say or do anything to change her behavior. "Sounds like a good idea. Go ahead and order a drink if you want to. I'll be there as soon as I can."

When Jen had insisted on coming up, he'd called his buddy Sean and asked for some nearby recommendations. While Boston boasted plenty of four- and five-star restaurants, driving in the city could be difficult and parking expensive. He didn't want to make Jen's trip any more inconvenient or costly. He knew she'd never accept an offer to pay for her parking. She wasn't that kind of woman.

Sean had come back with three suggestions. One had been right in North Salem, but it would've added at least twenty minutes to her drive, so he'd dismissed it right away. He'd checked the other two out before settling on Turin. He'd learned at some point that Italian was Jen's favorite food. Turin specialized in Italian and offered free onsite parking, something not all the restaurants in Salem had.

Brett picked the empty spot next to Jen's car. He managed to get halfway across the parking lot before his cell phone rang. The device had rung more in the past week than it had in the past year. A quick glance at the screen confirmed what he already knew; the caller was Carl. When he'd hired the man, Carl had joked he should just move into Brett's house since they'd be spending so much time together. He'd thought the guy was exaggerating, but after all the phone calls and lunch meetings they'd had this week alone, Brett realized how true the statement had been. It would probably only get worse the closer they got to the primary in November.

"Hi Carl," Brett said. "Now's not the best time. Can it wait until tomorrow?"

"I'll be quick tonight."

Carl's understanding of the word quick and his were worlds apart. A fact he'd learned this week when a "quick" lunch meeting turned into a two-hour affair.

"I just got word Ted Smith is on the November ballot. He turned his nomination papers in late this afternoon."

They'd already assumed the former lieutenant governor would be his main competition for the party nomination. In his mind, this news didn't change the strategy they'd developed. "Thanks for letting me know. Any other important updates?"

Brett stopped in front of the restaurant entrance. Any discussion they needed to have, he'd prefer to do it outside. Once he sat down, he wanted to devote his attention to Jen, not his campaign manager or the upcoming election.

"Not at the moment."

Thank you. Brett pulled open the door and stepped inside. "We'll talk later."

He shoved the device back into his pocket as he crossed the waiting area. Several people sat waiting for a table. Most were paying more attention to their electronic devices than each other or anyone else coming inside.

The hostess recognized him before he greeted her. He couldn't recall it ever happening to him before unless he'd been accompanied by one of his cousins. Even then it was his cousins people recognized, not him. "Mr. Sherbrooke, welcome to Turin. I've already seated your guest."

Brett forced a smile. *Better get used to this.* The first of his campaign television ads was scheduled to launch Monday. Once they did, his face would be even more recognizable. "Excellent. Thank you."

He followed the hostess through the candlelit dining room. As expected for a Friday night, all the tables were occupied. In here at least most of the people were having conversations with each other instead of texting away on their cell phones or checking their e-mails.

"Here we are, Mr. Sherbrooke." The hostess stopped at a table designed for two.

At the sound of the woman's voice, Jen looked up from her cell phone and a welcoming smile spread across her face. She didn't hesitate to put the device down.

Even though the hostess stood there, he walked around the table and brushed his lips across Jen's cheek before taking his seat.

"Ann will be taking care of you this evening. She'll be right over." The hostess handed Brett a menu before walking away.

Jen's menu remained closed on the table alongside an untouched glass of white wine.

"Sorry again for being late."

"Don't worry about it. Was traffic bad tonight?" she asked. "I definitely hit a little leaving the city."

"Horrendous. The worst it's been all week. I should've left earlier."

"Getting out of Providence on a Friday is always worse than the rest of the week too, especially this time of year. It gets a little better in the winter when people aren't trying to go away for the weekend. Sometimes I work late to avoid it. I imagine it's even worse in Boston." She reached for her menu and opened it. "I haven't decided on a meal yet. Do you recommend anything?"

Brett watched the candlelight dance across her face, more interested in that than what entrees the menu contained. "This is my first time here. I asked a friend for some recommendations and decided on here because it specializes in Italian. We can check out the other ones he suggested another time." He opened his menu but didn't look at what was listed inside.

"You remembered Italian is my favorite. Why am I not surprised?" She gifted him with another smile. "I peeked at the menu when I first sat down. Everything sounds amazing. I don't know how I'm going to decide."

"I think you should go with lasagna or baked stuffed shells," Brett said remembering well their conversation at Ambrosia about her dislike of ricotta cheese.

Jen looked up from the menu. "Since I know you're joking, I'm going to forget you even said that." She went back to reading the dishes available. "What are you considering?"

You. He wisely kept the thought to himself and finally glanced at his open menu. "No idea. I've had lasagna and fettuccini alfredo already this week. Carl's favorite restaurant is in the North End. We've met there twice for lunch."

"You should've made a reservation somewhere else tonight. I do enjoy other types of food."

"Why? Italian is one of my favorites too. And it's not like there aren't plenty of options on the menu."

Neither spoke again as they read over the dishes available and placed their orders. Only when the waitress left did Jen start a conversation.

"How was your first week at Homeland?" she asked.

"Different."

"Different good or different bad?"

Brett thought for a moment. He'd both enjoyed and disliked the hours he'd spent at his new job. "Both. I'm not used to sitting behind a desk so much. I guess I'll get used to it."

"It's not for everyone. Keith would go nuts in a chair all day."

He agreed. Her brother would start climbing the walls if stuck in an office.

"Any updates on the—"

Brett saw the man walking their way but didn't think anything of it until he stopped a few inches from their table. "Sorry to interrupt, but I wanted to introduce myself. City councilman Jeff Murphy," he said, cutting Jen off midsentence. He extended his hand toward Brett and continued, "I represent Salem's third ward. I'm also the chairman for the community and economic development subcommittee."

He'd hoped to leave politics at home, but it looked like that had been an unrealistic expectation tonight. "Nice to meet you." He shook the councilman's hand. "Brett Sherbrooke."

The man actually chuckled when Brett introduced himself. He interpreted the reaction to mean it'd been not only an unnecessary move but, at least in the councilman's eyes, a silly one.

Unsure of how Jen would want to be introduced to the unwelcome visitor, he said, "And this is my friend Jennifer."

"Very nice to meet you too," the councilman extended his

hand in Jen's direction. After shaking Jen's hand, he turned his full attention back to Brett. "I want you to know you have my full support in the primary." The councilman opened his wallet and pulled out a crisp white business card. "Don't hesitate to contact me if I can help you in any way."

This might be his first trip into politics, but he knew help from other politicians often came with strings attached. "Thank you for your support. I appreciate it." How many times had he read or heard Uncle Warren say that during his various campaigns? "I'll keep you in mind." He took the business card and dropped it into his shirt pocket.

The councilman smiled and nodded. "Enjoy your evening. Turin is one of our city's finest establishments. My wife and I are frequent visitors."

Brett watched the man walk away and rejoin a woman seated across the dining room. "I apologize for that too," he said. "Tonight isn't starting off well."

Jen reached for his hand. "You had about as much control over his visit as you did the traffic tonight. No need to apologize." She tilted her head in the councilman's general direction. "Before our unexpected visitor showed up, I was going to ask how the campaign is going."

They'd discussed the campaign a bit during their phone calls this week, but he'd made a conscious effort not to bore her with all the details. "Going as planned so far. I've got two town hall forums this week. One is Tuesday out in Amherst and the other is Wednesday in Boston. Thursday I have a meet and greet down in Westport." Brett proceeded to fill her in on the rest of his upcoming week.

JUST HEARING him list all the meetings and interviews filling his calendar made her tired. "So basically you have something scheduled for every day next week," she said after the waitress set down their main dishes. "How are you going to manage all that and work?"

"Creative scheduling as well as a lot of late nights and early mornings." He placed his napkin on his lap and picked up his fork. "This looks amazing. If it tastes as good as it looks, I'll have to thank Sean for telling me about this restaurant."

Jen followed his lead and picked up her fork as well. She agreed, the osso buco she'd ordered looked and smelled divine. "And when do you plan on sleeping?"

"After I win the election." He sounded a little too serious for her peace of mind.

"I'm not joking." She sliced a corner off her braised veal shank and waited for his reply.

Brett's hand paused with his fork almost to his mouth. "I wasn't either. You'd be surprised how little sleep a body can get by on."

Jen understood and respected his ambition, but no one could keep up the pace he was facing and stay healthy. "Brett, everyone needs some downtime. And I don't mean just sleep. Some time to relax and unwind is important too." She put her fork down because dinner could wait. This was a serious discussion. "You're no different. I think you need to take a step back for a minute. Perhaps consider taking a leave of absence from Homeland. I think they'd understand considering the circumstances."

His expression became grim, and he stopped eating. "Carl made a similar suggestion over lunch yesterday. I'll keep it in mind."

He sounded sincere, but for some reason she got the impression he was simply telling her what she wanted to hear. "Promise?"

Brett nodded, but she wasn't quite ready to let him off the hook. In many ways, Brett was like her dad and brother. They were all stubborn men who did things their way no matter anyone's opinion.

"Do you pinkie promise?"

Bella had asked her the same thing Sunday. Before Jen left with Bo, Bella had made her pinkie promise to let the dog stay with her again soon.

"A pinkie promise sounds serious." His hand slipped over hers. "And not something I'd enter into with just anyone." A grin broke free and overtook his features. "But I'll do it for you."

Jen raised the pinkie finger on her free hand and held it toward him. When he merely reached for his fork again, she said, "Aren't you forgetting something?"

"I don't think so."

She wiggled her finger in the air, assuming he'd catch on.

"Something wrong with your finger?" he asked instead.

She thought she caught a twinkle of laughter in his eyes, but at the same time it might only be the candle flame playing tricks on her. "A proper pinkie promise entails joining our fingers. Now let's see your finger, unless you didn't mean what you said."

Brett met her demand and linked his finger with hers. "In case you hadn't already figured this out, I always mean what I say."

His words sent a shiver of excitement down her spine. His voice told her he wasn't referring to just his promise to consider taking a leave from his job until after the election.

JEN TOOK a third bite of her dessert and pushed the plate away. "This is amazing, but I can't eat another bite." She shouldn't have ordered dessert in the first place. Her dinner had more than filled her up. When the waitress brought the tray over, her sweet tooth had taken over and prompted her to order the limoncello panna cotta with wild blueberry glaze despite her better judgment.

Across the table, Brett's dessert was already more than half gone. Exactly where he managed to put all the food was a mystery. Unlike her, he'd finished his main meal before indulging in the large chocolate torte he ordered.

"Any ideas of how you'd like to spend the rest of the night?" Brett asked, his fork already heading for his plate and the last piece of his dessert.

"If it was a little earlier and I had on more comfortable shoes, I'd say walk around the city. This is my first time to Salem." She'd come straight from work. Although she wasn't wearing heels—she rarely did—the sling-back flats she had one were not designed for long, leisurely strolls.

"First? You've never come up at Halloween time?"

"Nope. Until I moved to Rhode Island ten years ago, I didn't spend much time in New England. When I did come, it was usually at Christmas to see my grandparents."

Brett signed the bill their waitress handed him. "This October we'll have to rectify that. Salem embraces Halloween like no other place I know. All set?"

Come October he'd be neck-deep in his campaign. Finding time for them to meet and visit the city might be out of the question. While she recognized this, she kept it to herself. "Similar to the way New Orleans celebrates Mardi Gras?" she asked, pushing her chair back.

"I don't think any city or town in the country embraces a holiday the way New Orleans does when it comes to Mardi Gras." He put his arm around her waist and started toward the exit. "Experienced it once, and that was enough for me. Halloween in Salem, though, I could do again."

He filled her in on the events he'd seen on his one visit to Salem during October. From the sound of it, the city used the infamous witch trials held centuries ago and the hauntings associated with them to its advantage. Even if they didn't make it back in October together, perhaps she'd recruit Kristen and spend a day up here. Her sister was always up for a little exploring, and they hadn't had a girls' day out together in months.

"Walking is out for the night. Anything else you want to do?" Brett stopped next to her car.

Nothing came to mind, especially not still wearing the wraparound rayon dress she'd worn to work. She hated to see the evening end though. Brett had a ridiculously busy week ahead of him, so who knew when he might have time to see her again.

"Sorry, no, not dressed like this." She gestured toward her outfit. "You?"

The lights in the parking lot made it impossible to miss the way Brett's gaze left her face and roamed over her figure. He took a step closer, and the air between them danced with excitement. "I don't live far from here. Come to my house. We can watch a movie, talk, whatever." Brett ran a finger down her jaw and across her bottom lip, and her heart jerked against her rib cage.

She had a good idea of what the "whatever" might encompass. If it were any other man standing there and asking her back to his place after only technically two dates, she'd be jumping in her car and leaving him in the dust. Brett she knew perhaps better than any other man she'd ever dated. "I'll follow you."

Brett's car turned onto a street named Fender Drive. Although several businesses lined the street, including a grocery store and an automotive garage, the area radiated a small town vibe. As they passed through an intersection, the streetlights provided enough illumination for her to see the large town common. The streetlights ended though when Brett turned left. Now the only light came from the homes lining the street and her car's headlights.

In front of her, Brett stopped and turned. Jen waited until Brett pulled into his garage before turning into the driveway. The colonial-style home resembled many of the homes in her neighborhood, only this one looked to be much older. Actually, all the homes they'd passed on the street looked on the older side, and she wouldn't be surprised to find some had historical markers on the front.

Jen pushed open the car door as Brett approached. The sensor light attached to the garage made it possible to see the frown he wore. "What's wrong?" Had he noticed a problem with the house? Even small towns experienced break-ins and vandalism.

He tilted his head in the direction of the car door. "I was going to get it for you."

"Why?"

"Because I wanted to."

She closed the door and added her keys to her purse. "Next time." She looked around the front yard, her gaze stopping on the large front porch. "I love porches like that," she said. "One of the houses I lived in growing up had one. I used to sit outside and read out there even when it rained. Sometimes in the summer we'd eat breakfast out there on the weekends."

Brett's arm wrapped around her waist. Together they walked up the driveway and into the two-car garage. "We'll have to do that sometime." He pressed the control panel on the wall to close the garage door and unlocked the interior door.

Jen expected to walk into a kitchen. Most homes, hers included, seemed to have a door in the kitchen that led directly into the garage. However, she hadn't expected to walk into an empty kitchen. The only evidence someone lived there was the overly complicated looking coffee maker on the counter. There was no kitchen table or chairs. The counters gleamed as if recently washed. There wasn't a single item in the sink, not even a dirty spoon. No matter how hard she tried, she always seemed to find a stray utensil or empty glass in her kitchen sink. The glass doors on the cabinets above the counter revealed that most were empty. Only the one closest to the stove contained any dishes. The cabinet doors below the counter weren't glass, so she didn't know what was behind those, but if she opened them she didn't think she'd find anything.

"I thought your things arrived?" she asked.

"They did, and I finished unpacking." He led her through the spotless kitchen and into another room. "Make yourself at home." He left her side long enough to turn on more lights.

Although not as empty as the kitchen, this room didn't contain much furniture either. "Did they leave some of it in Virginia?"

The leather sofa looked comfortable and high-end. Definitely not something he'd picked up at a discount furniture store. However, it and the large square coffee table were the only things in the room, unless you counted the huge flat-screen television mounted over the fireplace. The room could easily accommodate a few armchairs and an end table or two.

"Nope. I didn't have a lot, just the essentials."

"You consider a sixty-five-inch television more essential than a kitchen table?" she asked, guessing at the size of the television. At home she had a forty-inch mounted on the wall, and Brett's was much larger than it.

He took the remote from the coffee table and switched on the obnoxiously large device mounted on the wall. "Affirmative. A movie or football game on anything smaller is a waste of time."

Only a man would consider a television more important than a table. "You sound like my brother."

He brought up his movie collection. "I'll prove it to you. Pick anything you want." Brett gestured with the remote. "But don't worry, I'll get around to buying more furniture, including a kitchen table. My sister offered, but we have different tastes."

She wondered what else the house was lacking. If she walked into his bedroom, would she find a sleeping bag on the floor? "Okay, if you say so. You're the one who has to stand up while he eats breakfast, not me."

Jen didn't wait for him, instead she sat down on the sofa. "Let's test your opinion. What movies do we have to pick from?"

He sat down too, his thigh rubbing against hers, and put an arm across her shoulders. "Take a look and pick whatever you want." He handed her the remote and then undid the top two buttons on his shirt.

She scrolled through the various movies, not at all surprised by what she found. Except for horror films, they liked all the same kind of movies. She'd never understood the appeal of horror movies or even books. What was so entertaining about being scared to death? She'd watched a few in college and then spent several nights sleeping with her dorm room light on and jumping at every single sound.

"I've got two in mind. Do you prefer *A New Hope* or the first *Lord of the Rings*?"

The fabric of his pants rubbed against her thigh, pulling her gaze to his long legs as he stretched them out. Many of the men she'd dated in the past had either been her height, or in one instance slightly shorter. She found it nice to be with someone taller than her for a change.

"Whichever will keep you here longer." His breath drifted over her skin, leaving a trail of goose bumps behind before he kissed her cheek.

"We could always watch both." She turned her head and met his eyes, the desire she saw in them kicking up the sensual excitement already humming inside her.

His gaze dropped to her lips before meeting her eyes again. "If it keeps you here all night, we can do that." Brett touched her lips with his. It was the gentlest kiss she'd ever had, yet her pulse quickened and unimaginable wanting ran through her.

No one was expecting her at home, not even her dog. Before

she drove to Salem, she'd stopped home to let Bo out and feed him. Since Kristen lived only a few miles away, she'd promised to visit after the family finished dinner. If Jen wasn't home yet she'd take him back to her house. There was nothing to stop her from spending the whole night here.

She pulled her mouth away so she could speak. "Or we could find another way to entertain ourselves."

Jen caught the spark in his eyes before she kissed the side of his neck. She made a path across his skin until her lips closed around her earlobe; then she gently raked her teeth across it. Brett's soft groan reached her ears moments before he untied the knot on the side of her dress and pushed the material open. When his hand touched her bare skin, she sucked in a deep breath. She'd barely managed to exhale, when he cupped her breast and at the same time set his lips against hers.

CHAPTER 6

BRETT WATCHED Jen pull his New England Rebels T-shirt over her head.

"I was worried I'd find a sleeping bag on your bedroom floor," she said.

"Bull." He dug a pair of shorts out of his drawer and put them on. He didn't bother with a shirt.

"I'm not kidding. I thought maybe beds fell into the nonessential category along with kitchen tables."

He walked around the king-size bed. Although a queen would fit better in this room, he hated sleeping in anything smaller unless he had no other choice. "Believe it or not, I have two in the house." He pointed to the bed next to Jen. "I got this one after I bought the house so I'd have a place to sleep when I visited. The mattress from my old condo is in one of the other bedrooms."

The house had three bedrooms in addition to the master. None of them were huge, but all were a decent size.

Stepping closer, Jen linked her arms around his waist. His body reacted immediately to the feel of her hands on his skin. "Maybe there is some hope for you?" She kissed him before moving back. "I think it's time to test your opinion of televisions. Ready for a movie?"

He'd rather they get into bed and go back to finding other ways to entertain themselves. But if she wanted to watch a movie, he'd do it. "You'll see I'm right."

In the living room, Jen picked her dress up from the floor and folded it before sitting down. "Any preference?" she asked, reaching for the remote they'd left on the table.

"Whatever you want. I'll be right back."

In the kitchen, he took two bottles of iced tea from the fridge. "Hungry?" he called. When he watched a movie, he needed a snack. It didn't matter if it'd been only five minutes or five hours since his last meal. If a movie was playing, he needed to munch on preferably something salty, but in a pinch cookies worked too.

"Nope."

Brett opened the kitchen closet. Popcorn would be nice, but since he didn't have any, the roasted peanuts would do. Before leaving the room, he grabbed the cell phone he'd left on the counter earlier. He wasn't expecting any calls, but you never knew with Carl. Thursday the man had called him close to midnight.

He handed Jen the open bottle of iced tea and sat down next to her. "If you change your mind, let me know." The opening paragraph to *A New Hope* scrolled across the screen as the recognizable music filled the room. He'd read the words enough times he could recite them from memory. "Any plans for tomorrow?" He had no free time next week, so he wanted to spend as much time with her this weekend as he could.

"I do have a hot date with my washing machine planned, but I can probably reschedule. I don't think he'd mind."

"You'd do that for me?"

Jen nodded. "But only this once. I can't make a habit of it. He might get jealous."

"Tomorrow night there's a block party on the town common. I have no idea what to expect. It might be awful. My buddy told me the town holds one every month starting in the spring. Tomorrow's the last one until next year. He said there is usually food, music, and dancing." Food and music he enjoyed. Dancing he only did if left with no other option, like when his sister dragged him on the dance floor at their cousin's wedding in June. "Any interest in checking it out?"

"Sure, sounds like it could be fun." She took a sip from her iced tea and then set the bottle down on the coffee table. "What time does it start?"

Good question. He hadn't asked. "I don't know. The town's website should have it listed. It lists everything else." He'd visited the site a handful of times and found information regarding every aspect of the town. "I can come pick you up sometime in the afternoon. Bring your dog too, and you can stay the night."

A mischievous grin spread across her face. "Well, it's not like you have much Bo could destroy in here."

He knew she was only joking, but maybe he should do something about getting more furniture and stuff. "I don't suppose you want to handle decorating this place for me?"

His sister would turn the house into a mini replica of hers with no regard to his preferences. However, he'd seen the inside of Jen's house. Her style was much more in line with what he liked, and he hated shopping.

Her expression grew serious. "Brett, I'm just kidding. This is your house. As long as you're comfortable here that's all that matters."

"If I'm going to live here and have visitors, it does need more stuff. Leah offered, but she'll turn it into a place I'm afraid to walk in without taking my shoes off first. What do you say? Do you want to take my credit card and go on a shopping spree?"

"Thanks but no thanks. But I will go and help you. I'll even hang curtains if you want."

He'd rather she took his card and bought what she thought he needed. He put shopping and visiting the doctor in the same category. Both were necessary from time to time, but he never enjoyed either.

"I'll take it. But back to what we were talking about. It's up to you, but I'd love to have you spend the night tomorrow. The backyard is fenced in, so Bo can run around out there if he needs to, or just hang around in here."

"Are you sure? My sister would take him again for me."

"I always mean what I say." He'd told her the same thing in the restaurant, but it didn't hurt to say it again now.

"Okay, but you don't have to come pick me up. I can drive back tomorrow."

Jen said her sister would take the dog again; did that mean Bo was with her tonight? Since she appeared to be in no rush to get home, it seemed likely. "Is Bo at your sister's tonight?"

Jen nodded and several strands of hair fell forward. She pushed them back before she answered him. "I didn't know how late I'd be. Kristen only lives a few miles away from me, so she picked him up after dinner. My niece loves it when Bo spends the night, and she does most of the work."

If her dog wasn't waiting for her at home, he saw no reason she couldn't stay here tonight too. "Then stay tonight. Tomorrow we can drive to your house together. Get a change of clothes, your dog, and come back."

It'd been a damn long time since he woke up in the morning with a woman next to him. Sure he'd had a handful of women in his bed over the last few years, but he hadn't asked or wanted a single one of them to stay the night. Jen was nothing like any of those women. He not only wanted her in his bed, he wanted her involved in every aspect of his life too.

JEN WRAPPED her dress around her body and tied it before running her fingers through her hair. Without a brush or comb handy, it was the best she could do. At least she wouldn't be seeing anyone this morning. Before leaving the bedroom, she made Brett's bed and tossed the T-shirt he'd let her borrow for the night into the laundry basket. If she'd been at home, there was a fifty-fifty chance she would've left it on the bed where she'd first dropped it, but it didn't take an advanced degree in astrophysics to know Brett liked things neat and tidy. She'd gotten a peek in his underwear drawer when he got dressed this morning. Even in there everything had been folded neatly and stacked in piles. Towels and jeans she folded. Underwear got dumped in a pile in her drawer.

The scent of strong coffee reached her before she entered the kitchen.

"I think I prefer you dressed the other way," Brett said when she walked in.

She preferred him any old way.

"Coffee?"

"Yes, please." She yawned as she crossed to where he stood leaning with his back against the counter.

He took down a mug from the cabinet by the stove and filled it. "There's milk in the fridge."

She grabbed the plastic half gallon, glad to see he had plenty of fresh fruit and vegetables inside. She'd worried his fridge might be as empty as the kitchen cabinets appeared to be. "Thank you." Jen reached for the mug, but he pulled it back before she touched it.

"It's going to cost you."

Crossing her arms, she narrowed her eyes at him. "Oh, really?"

Brett set both mugs down and advanced on her. "I made you coffee, I think that deserves at least a good morning kiss."

She'd kissed him on the cheek before he got out of bed. If he wanted another, she'd oblige. Jen brushed her lips across his cheek. "Okay, I paid. Now hand over the goods." She tried to reach around him to get her mug, but he blocked her attempt.

"Not so fast. I want a proper kiss, not whatever that was."

If she'd brushed her teeth or at the very least used some mouthwash, she'd treat him to the same type of kisses they'd shared last night. She hadn't come prepared for a sleepover and hadn't wanted to go snooping through the drawers in the bathroom. "What you have in mind will have to wait until we get to my house, and I brush my teeth."

Brett reached behind him and picked up her coffee. "Sorry, can't wait until then. Don't worry, I've got plenty of extra toothbrushes. Enjoy your coffee, and I'll get you one."

Did he have extra toothbrushes in the house because he invited a lot of women to spend the night or simply because he liked to be prepared? In none of the letters or text messages they'd exchanged had he ever mentioned a girlfriend, and she only remembered him once saying something about going on a blind date set up by a friend.

"You don't have kitchen chairs to sit on but you've got extra toothbrushes hanging around?"

"It's all about what's essential." He took a gulp from his coffee before setting it back down. "Instead of subjecting you to my cooking, I thought we could pick something up on the way. There's a nice café in town. It makes great breakfast sandwiches and muffins."

When Brett backed out of the driveway twenty minutes later, the dancing baby pink and blue balloons attached to his neighbors' mailbox immediately caught her attention. Usually there was only one reason people had those color balloons outside their home.

"Looks like your neighbors had twins," she said, pointing toward the house next door.

"I saw Jessie in the driveway earlier this week. She looked miserable and about ready to pop."

At one time, she'd thought having twins would be great. Then her sister had Bella and she saw how much work just one baby could be. She couldn't imagine having two infants at the same time. "Do they have any other children?" If Brett's neighbors had more, she hoped they were at least school aged.

He put the SUV, one of the essentials the movers had delivered the previous week, in drive and drove down the street. "Yeah, a little girl. No idea how old she is. I've only met her once, but she seemed like a nice kid. They've got a dog too."

After a quick stop at Peggy Sue's Café, a cute little place on what seemed to be the main street in and out of town, they got on the highway. When she'd made the trip up this way last night, traffic had been on the heavy side as people headed north for the weekend. This morning though they cruised along without any backups and made what the GPS said should be an hour and thirty-minute drive in about an hour and fifteen minutes.

She waved back at Marie, her next-door neighbor, as she and Brett walked toward her front door. Recently retired, Marie and her husband had raised their family in the house next door and she loved to work in her yard. More times than not, Jen found her, and often her husband, doing some type of yard project. If she were outside when they were, she'd usually chat. This morning she'd prefer to skip a conversation, because although very nice, Marie tended to be a little long-winded and sometimes nosy.

"Make yourself at home. I'm going to take a quick shower." She'd considered taking one at Brett's after brushing her teeth, but it had seemed silly to do so and then put back on the same underwear she'd worn all day yesterday.

"Take your time. No need to rush."

In her room, Jen sent off a quick text message letting her sister know she'd be over soon to pick up Bo and kicked her shoes off at the same time. She didn't wait around for a response. Instead she tossed the cell phone on her bed and headed for the bathroom. Brett may not care how long she took, but she hated to keep anyone waiting.

The opening theme song to a movie greeted her when she walked into her bedroom a few minutes later. She'd told Brett to make himself at home; if he'd turned on the television downstairs, he'd obviously done just that. Jen searched through her drawer for a top. A town block party sounded pretty casual; still, she didn't want to look like a complete slob. She skipped over several shirts before settling on the new red off-the-shoulder blouse she'd picked up during her last trip to the mall. It'd be cool enough for a warm summer night outside but not as casual as a plain old T-shirt. "Now for tomorrow," she said, digging her duffle bag out of her closet. She didn't travel much, and the bag was buried under a pile of shoes and a bag of clothes she kept meaning to donate.

The cell phone on her nightstand beeped as she dropped the duffle bag on her bed. Jen picked it up and walked back to the chest of drawers for clothes.

Get here whenever. Bella is playing fetch with Bo in the yard. Can't wait to hear about last night.

Any discussion about last night would have to wait until another time. They couldn't discuss her date with Brett standing next to them. Jen grabbed a pair of shorts from a drawer.

Dan's parents and Mom and Dad are coming over. We're going to have a cookout. You're welcome too. A second message from Kristen appeared before Jen answered the first.

Normally she'd accept such an invitation. This morning she typed back a simple *thank you*. She and Brett had a limited amount of time together. She loved her family, but she wasn't sure she wanted to include them into their weekend plans. That was of course assuming Brett would be open to meeting Mom and Dad today. Men could be weird about that kind of thing. Some saw it as a big step toward the whole ball and chain and avoided it at all costs. She didn't want to do anything this weekend that would make him uncomfortable or cause him to think she expected a diamond ring.

"All set." Jen walked into the living room and found Brett with his cell phone pressed against his ear and the movie paused.

"I'll have to get back to you," he said before ending the call.

"Did something come up?" she asked. Their plans to spend the night together had been last-minute, and he was in the middle of running for Senate. She'd be disappointed but would understand if unexpected campaign stuff cut into their time today.

He switched off the television as he stood. "No, it was just my uncle. My cousin Allison and her boyfriend got engaged last night. Uncle Mark and his wife are throwing them a little engagement party before Allison and Rock go back to Virginia. He called to invite me." Brett shoved the cell phone into a pocket.

Oh well, sounded like their weekend plans were about to change. She knew family was as important to him as it was to her. He wouldn't want to skip an engagement party for his cousin regardless of how short notice it had been.

"I'm sure you'll have fun." Should she pick Bo up and bring him back here before she went back to Brett's and got her car? Or should she go get her car and grab Bo on her way home? Bo had been with her sister since last night; it would be more considerate if she went and picked him up first and brought him home before making the round-trip to North Salem and back.

"Do you mind if we pick up Bo and bring him back here before we go back to your house so I can get my car?"

"You changed your mind about staying with me tonight?" He rounded the sofa and came to stand near her.

Jen shook her head. "No, but I thought you'd want to see your family."

"The party's tomorrow afternoon. And if you can reschedule with your washing machine again, I'd like you to come."

An informal cookout like her sister was having was one thing. This engagement party sounded like a big deal. "Are you sure someone won't mind you bringing an uninvited guest?"

"It'll only be my family, Rock's parents, and maybe his oldest brother. I'm not even sure if his other two are stateside right now." He wrapped a hand over each of her shoulders. "If you'd rather skip it though we can. It's not a big deal if I miss it. Uncle Mark knows not everyone will make it on such short notice. And Allison will understand if I don't get there."

Upstairs she'd been worried about asking Brett to meet her parents and now he wanted to her to meet most of his family. Evidently, she'd worried for nothing. "If you want, I'll come, but I'll need to repack before we leave. How formal is this party going to be?"

His cousin Derek had come across as down-to-earth, but tomorrow she'd be surrounded by some of society's most elite individuals. The old cutoffs and T-shirt in her bag wouldn't cut it.

Brett gave her a smile bright enough to light up her entire house. "Outstanding. But don't stress about your clothes. It's at Uncle Mark's house, so nothing formal."

The man he kept calling Uncle Mark was also supreme court chief justice in Rhode Island. Someone with a title like that wouldn't throw a party where cutoffs were acceptable. "I'll be right back."

She started to turn but stopped when she remembered they planned to take Bo with them back to Brett's house. His uncle might not mind an extra human guest, but a four-legged one might not go over so well. She opened her mouth to speak, but didn't get the opportunity.

"Already figured it, so don't worry," he said. "Tomorrow I'll follow you here. You can drop off the dog, and we can drive over to my uncle's together. The party is at his house in Barrington. After the party, I'll bring you home and drive back to North Salem."

How had he'd known what she was thinking? "Do you have some special minding reading abilities you never told me about?"

He moved into her personal space again. "Just good at planning and carrying out missions." Brett gave her a kiss. "My current mission is introducing you to my family."

BRETT PARKED behind the same minivan he'd seen at Jen's house the previous weekend and a silver sedan. "You do live close to your sister." It had taken them less than ten minutes to get from Jen's to her sister's.

"Before Kristen got her current job, she traveled a fair amount for work. Dan is a basketball coach at Providence College so he travels like crazy, especially during basketball season. I bought a house nearby so I could help her out." She picked her purse up off the floor and reached for the door handle. "Mom and Dad live within walking distance. Bella goes there every day after school until Kristen gets home from work."

He'd seen a picture of who he guessed were Jen's parents in her living room. She didn't resemble either of them. There'd also been a copy of the same picture she'd sent him. While Jen didn't resemble the couple in the photo, her brother Keith and sister Kristen did. There had also been a photo of a young girl with hair so blonde it almost looked white. Although the hair and eyes were different from Kristen's, the girl looked enough like her mother that Bret knew it was Jen's niece.

The same girl from the photo answered the door after Jen

rang the bell. "Hey, Auntie Jen." The girl glanced in his direction and gave him a look that said, "Who are you and what are you doing here?"

"Hey sweetie. Thanks for taking care of Bo last night." Jen hugged her niece and kissed her cheek before looking back at him. "Brett, this is my niece, Bella. She always does a fantastic job of taking care of Bo."

Jen had told him Bella was ten. How did you greet a ten-year-old girl? A handshake seemed over the top. A hug would be inappropriate, and he certainly couldn't salute her. "Hello."

She treated him to another piercing glance, and he wondered if she led a secret life as a police interrogator. "Hi," she finally said before looking back at her aunt. "Are you staying for the cookout?"

"Uh, I'm not sure." Jen didn't sound surprised by the invitation.

"Mom got stuff to make s'mores, and Gram is bringing brownies."

Jen looked at him and then took his hand. "We'll think about it. Where's your mom?"

"In the kitchen, and Dad's in the backyard." A song he didn't recognize erupted from the tablet in Bella's hands. "It's Gretchen. She's getting a dog today," she said before taking off up the stairs.

Brett didn't know how much longer they'd be alone, so before she led him into the kitchen, he said, "Did you know about the cookout?"

"Kristen invited me this morning. I wasn't sure if you'd want to stick around for it or not."

"If there'll be s'mores and brownies around, I'm game."

"And my parents. My brother-in-law's parents are coming too."

He failed to see a problem. "You're going to meet my

parents tomorrow. I'll leave the decision up to you. Just keep in mind there will be brownies available."

Jen gave him a slight nudge in the side. "Wow, you *do* have a sugar problem. Have you considered getting help?"

"Hey, I warned you I had a sweet tooth. Don't act shocked now."

"In that case, we better stay so you don't go into sugar with-drawal or something on me. Come on. Let's go tell Kristen we're staying."

They found Bo, Jen's dog, in the kitchen. He sat on the floor near Kristen's feet. As she worked, his eyes remained focused on the counter and the chicken Kristen was sliding onto kabob sticks.

"Hi Kristen," Jen said, walking in the room. Immediately Bo left Kristen's side and walked over to them. "How's my boy?"

Jen bent down to pet the dog and missed the look of surprise on her sister's face. Brett didn't. Whatever conversation Jen had with her sister earlier, she hadn't mentioned they were still together this morning.

Kristen washed her hands and walked toward them. "Hi Brett." She extended her hand and smiled. "It's nice to see you again." Kristen shot a look toward Jen who was again standing up straight.

Brett nodded. "You too."

She glanced at Jen again. "You're welcome to stay. There's enough food. Mom and Dad should be here soon."

"We'll stay for a little while. Do you need any help?" Jen answered.

Kristen wanted to grill her sister. He saw it in the woman's expression. Instead she nodded toward the fridge. "If you don't mind, the peppers need to be washed and cut up."

Brett offered to help as well, but Kristen immediately turned him down. Since his cooking skills sucked, it was probably just as well. Instead he took a seat at the kitchen table and watched the two women. It was a bit like watching the odd couple work together. While Jen was tall with strawberry-blonde hair, her sister was just the opposite. If he had to make a guess, he'd say Kristen topped out at five feet, and she had light brown hair. He hadn't met Dan, Jen's brother-in-law, yet. Since Bella had such light hair, he assumed the guy must be a blond or something close to it.

At the counter Kristen whispered something. Up until then, he'd heard all of the women's conversation. Whatever she'd just said, he wasn't meant to hear. In response, Jen shook her head and then walked back to the fridge. "Brett, do you want some lemonade?" She glanced back over at him.

"No thanks."

Jen poured herself a glass and was about to put the glass pitcher away when a man walked in from outside.

"Hey, Jen. Kristen said she invited you." The man gave Jen a brief hug and grabbed the pitcher from her hand. "I'm glad you're staying." He looked in Brett's direction and then back to Jen.

"Dan, this is Brett."

He didn't miss Jen's brief pause before she said his name. She wasn't sure how to label him. He'd have to clear that up later.

"Brett, my brother-in-law, Dan." She gestured toward the blond man. "And the best grill chef in the world."

"Keep giving me compliments like that and Bo can stay here anytime," Dan said, before turning his attention in Brett's direction. "Nice to meet you." He set the lemonade back in the fridge and pulled out a beer. "Can I get you one?" Dan held up the bottle.

Brett didn't recognize the label, but he wasn't picky. "Sounds good."

~

SHE LOOKED out the kitchen window. Brett was sitting and talking with her family. Even Bo was with them. The dog had parked himself near Brett's feet after Bella stopped feeding him pieces of her chicken.

"Since you showed up with him this morning, I'm assuming last night went well," Kristen said. She stood at the counter loading the dishes Jen rinsed into the dishwasher.

Jen handed her sister another plate. "Very."

"What, no other details?"

"Nope. But we do have plans for tonight too. There's a town block party where he lives. We won't be able to stay here much longer. And tomorrow we're going to his cousin's engagement party."

She swallowed at the thought of meeting his family. It'd been a long time since she met even a boyfriend's parents, never mind his aunts and uncles. Actually, now that she thought about it, she'd never had a boyfriend introduce her to his extended family.

Kristen added the last plate to the machine and closed the door. "Sounds like this relationship is at warp speed five." Much like Jen, Kristen was a bit of sci-fi geek. "He looks pretty comfortable out there with Mom and Dad. With Dan and his parents too."

She nodded and watched him laugh at something Dad said. "He does. Bella has even warmed up to him." Before lunch and even during, her niece had sat and studied him, her expression surprisingly serious for a ten-year-old. Now she sat between him and Dan with a smile on her face.

"If you need us to take Bo again tonight, we will. Bella loves having him here. You know for her it's the next best thing to having a dog of her own."

"Is Dan still making her wait until she's eleven?" Jen understood her brother-in-law wanting to wait until Bella was old enough to handle the responsibility of having a pet. However, she thought Bella had watched Bo enough in the past year to prove she could handle it.

"I think he's starting to reconsider, but don't tell Bella I said that. She'll start hounding us even more."

"My lips are sealed," Jen said. "If you don't mind, maybe I will leave him here again. Brett told me to take him back with us, but it might be better if Bo stays here. He's familiar with this house."

Kristen had started to uncover the brownies, but she paused. "You're spending the night at his house?"

She moved closer and peeked over her shoulder at the door. "I stayed there last night." Jen kept her voice low even though there was no way anyone would overhear her.

Her sister's eyes grew big. "You are moving fast." She looked out the window again. "Sometime this week we need to have a nice long chat without Bella or Dan around so you can fill me in on all the details."

Jen was closer to Kristen than anyone else in the world. "I'll call you." She tugged the plate closer and finished unwrapping the brownies. "We better get these desserts out there before the natives get restless and storm the castle. Brett's sweet tooth is worse than Dan's, if you can believe it." She'd known Dan long enough to know he ate healthy most of the time and worked out on a regular basis. However, he did love to indulge in the sweet stuff.

"No way. Not possible. If it weren't for me, the only green in Dan's diet would come from pistachio-flavored ice cream." Kristen gathered up the ingredients for making s'mores as well as the tray of oatmeal cookies her mother-in-law had brought. "But if you're right, Brett's waistline doesn't suffer because of it."

She'd noticed the same thing. "Tell me about it. Some things in life aren't fair. I look at a cookie and gain a pound. You should've seen the dessert he polished off last night."

Kristen walked toward the door. "Some people are just lucky that way."

She'd always been envious of her sister because Kristen definitely fell into the lucky category. The woman could indulge in pizza and a beer every day and not gain an ounce. She on the other hand had to be conscious of what she ate. She never obsessed about it, but she definitely needed to keep in mind how many times a month she indulged in a bowl of ice cream. Some months it was easier than others. She'd worried that over the summer she'd given in to temptation one too many times. Brett didn't seem to find anything wrong with her figure though, so maybe she'd been a little too critical of herself lately.

CHAPTER 7

A WOMAN DRESSED in black slacks and a white blouse answered the door and Phillip pasted on a smile. "Phillip Young. Mr. Smith is expecting me this afternoon."

"Yes, he mentioned you would be arriving," the woman said, taking a step back so Phillip could enter the house. "He's waiting in his office. Please follow me."

Phillip followed the woman through the two-story foyer and down a hallway. The moment Ted Smith had approached him about running his campaign, he'd done his homework. He knew the former lieutenant governor had gotten this home as well as the one in Vermont in the divorce. His ex-wife had gotten the home in the Hamptons and the one on Martha's Vineyard. He didn't know what the other houses looked like, but it didn't appear as though Ted Smith had suffered following the messy and very public divorce. The event would be the biggest obstacle standing between his client and the open Senate seat in Washington.

In front of him, the woman paused and knocked before opening the door. "Mr. Smith, your associate has arrived." She stepped back so Phillip could enter the room.

"Thank you, Lila," Ted said.

He left his spot behind his desk and met Phillip in the middle of the home office. "Nice to see you again. Have a seat." He gestured toward the small conference table in the room. "Can I get you anything to drink?"

When it came to alcohol, Phillip favored whiskey, but he'd drink anything. From the research he'd done, the same could be said about Ted. "Whatever you're having is fine."

While his new employer poured them drinks, Phillip set down his leather portfolio and laptop. The easy part had been getting the signatures necessary to get Ted on the ballot. If they had any hope of him winning first the primary and then the election, they had a lot of work to do. Especially considering whom he'd be up against in the primary.

Damn Sherbrookes. Anyone else and Phillip was confident the man before him could win even with his less than stellar past. However, running against a member of the Sherbrooke family made the possibility far less likely. Not that it would stop him from trying. When it came to running campaigns, Phillip had a reputation to maintain. And nothing was going to stand in his way of getting his candidate elected. Not even a member of the Sherbrooke family.

"Did you see the most recent polls?" Phillip asked once Ted sat down across from him.

"No, not yet. I haven't had a chance to check them."

That wasn't the answer he wanted to hear. If Ted was going to win, he needed to dedicate himself to this campaign, and that meant eating, sleeping, and drinking politics every day no matter what until November.

"As of this afternoon, the polls have Brett Sherbrooke ahead of you by ten points." He'd seen candidates overcome such deficits on occasion, but he'd prefer a much small margin. "Hammond and Reed are tied as of now. Neither of them are our concern at this point, however." After he helped Ted win the primary, he'd turn his attention to ruining the other party's candidate.

Ted sipped his drink as he mulled over the information. "All things considered, it's better than I expected. I'll be upfront with you. I thought I would have this race in the bag until I saw the Sherbrooke name." He took another sip before setting the glass down. "Between you and me, I'm not sure we can compete. He's got resources I don't."

Phillip glanced around the home office. He didn't have the man's bank records, but if this house was any indication, he was doing quite well despite the monthly alimony and child support payments he had to both his ex-wife and his former mistress. Today he wasn't here to discuss finances though. Those particulars he'd leave to Ted's finance coordinator.

"Sherbrooke might have an edge there, but he doesn't have the experience you do. Many won't care what his name is because he doesn't have the same political knowledge you do."

Perhaps he was stretching the truth somewhat. While Brett Sherbrooke hadn't held an office, he'd grown up around politicians. No one could spend that much time around politics and not learn a thing or two. Ted didn't need to hear that, especially not today. The man who'd first approached him to run his campaign had been confident and ready to tackle anyone who stood in his way. The man across the table this afternoon was giving off a very different vibe.

"It's not the only thing he doesn't have," Ted said before downing the rest of his drink.

The man's personal life was worthy of a drama series, however they'd discussed it already. While not ideal, Ted wasn't the first politician to have extramarital affairs surface. Ted also wasn't the first to have a secret baby come to light while going through an ugly divorce. He hadn't seemed overly concerned about any of it during their previous meetings. He did now.

"Is there anything else I need to know?" Phillip asked. When it came to running a campaign, he needed to know everything short of when the man across the table used the bathroom.

"My former personal assistant is pregnant. I found out last night. She's due the end of November."

He'd met the former Miss Massachusetts Ted was currently dating. She'd been at the house during their first meeting. He didn't think she could be six months pregnant. "Are you referring to Arianna?"

Ted walked away and refilled his tumbler. "No, that would be too easy. Victoria worked as my personal assistant for four or five months."

The man's personal life already resembled a bad reality show. They didn't need a pregnant former employee to add to the mix. "She waited long enough to tell you. Are you sure the baby is yours?"

Ted nodded. "As sure as I can be without a paternity test. The dates match up." He rejoined Phillip at the table. "She claims she's willing to keep the truth to herself as long as I agree to pay child support."

He'd seen too many people go back on such promises. If it did come out, they needed it to be after Ted won the Senate seat. "I recommend going along with whatever she wants. At least for now." Phillip reached for his untouched drink.

"It was my intention."

"And in the meantime, we need to try to dig up something we can use on Sherbrooke." Phillip considered himself an expert in that area. He'd dug up enough skeletons on various political candidates to fill a cemetery. He'd only failed once, while working on Richardson's presidential campaign in the last election.

"I don't see it happening. I've done my research too. Brett Sherbrooke has a reputation a Boy Scout would be jealous of. Add in his military background and family name and there's nothing we can use against him."

Phillip agreed. While working on Richardson's campaign he'd done everything he could to dig up something to use against then Senator Warren Sherbrooke. He'd even gotten intimately involved with Sherbrooke's younger daughter, Sara. He'd come up empty-handed. He didn't think they'd uncover anything useful now either, but he'd try.

"Let me do some digging into his background. If he doesn't have anything, then we just find something on someone close to him. A girlfriend perhaps." He hadn't heard Brett's name linked to anyone, but it didn't mean he wasn't involved with a woman —or a man for that matter. "Unless you object, I have contacts who can help with this particular project and be discreet."

"I want that Senate seat. Do whatever you have to do," Ted said.

CHAPTER 8

SHE FOLLOWED her dog outside and into Brett's backyard so he could have one last potty break. As soon as Brett finished his phone call, they were heading over to the town common for the block party. Before leaving Kristen's house, she'd considered leaving Bo there again for the night. Brett convinced her otherwise by pointing out it would be an extra stop she'd have to make at some point tomorrow. Bella had been disappointed but his argument made sense.

Jen sat in the only chair outside and waited as Bo took his time sniffing every blade of grass and leaf in the yard. From her seat, she could just make out the music being played at the party. When they'd driven by the area earlier, she'd seen workers setting up the inflatable bouncy houses, and she'd spotted the grills already there. North Salem might be a small town, but it looked like they went all out on their community events. She could understand why Brett had picked this town when he moved back to New England.

The door behind her opened, the sound catching Bo's attention. The dog paused in his investigation and looked to see who had joined them. When he saw it was only Brett, he went back to his sniffing again, only pausing long enough to lift his leg on every other spot.

"Sorry," Brett said, his hand coming down on her bare shoulder. "Carl wanted to fill me in on the newest polling results."

Political polls were not always 100 percent accurate, but they often proved true. "And how do things look?"

"They have me ahead of Ted Smith," he said, sounding neither disappointed nor thrilled by the news.

"Heck, even if I didn't know you, I'd vote for you over him. I remember hearing about all the affairs he had when he was lieutenant governor and getting a divorce. There were stories about questionable business deals too."

"His personal life aside, he's got the political experience I don't."

Political experience wasn't the only thing to consider, in her opinion. "Experience or not, he's still a scumbag. I don't know why anyone would vote for him."

Brett laughed. "Don't disagree with you there. The polls also have Gina Hammond and Vince Reed tied for their party's nomination."

Gina Hammond, the name sounded familiar. Jen searched her brain for it. "Hammond, isn't she from Vermont? I thought she ran for a Senate seat from there in a recent election."

"Was from Vermont. She lives in Cambridge now. I guess she thought she might have a better chance of winning in Massachusetts."

"Well that's sleazy. Moving from one state to another just to run for a political office."

Finished with his business, Bo joined them on the patio. Crouching down, Brett scratched the dog behind the ears. "Isn't that what I did?"

Open mouth, insert foot. "It's not the same. You didn't run for a Senate seat in Virginia and then move here after you lost so you could run again. She did."

Brett shrugged. "What Gina did is all part of the game, whether we like it or not." He stood up and held out his hand. "All set to head over?"

They crossed Brett's street and cut through the church parking to the horseshoe-shaped road that encircled the town common. People of all ages moved about the area and various scents filled the air. From here she could see the bouncy houses rocking as children jumped inside and a line of several others stood waiting their turn. A DJ was set up on the bandstand, cranking out hits. At the moment, he was playing a popular top forty hit she'd heard on the radio earlier in the week while getting a coffee. The one he'd played before though had been an oldie popular when her parents had been teens.

"This is quite the event," she said as they walked across the grass with no particular destination in mind. "I can't believe they throw something like this once a month all summer."

"Sean told me the town is big into community togetherness."

When you thought about all the terrible events happening in the world, she didn't think a little community spirit was a bad thing. "Maybe more places should try it."

"Maybe." He stopped walking and looked around. "Where to first? I know the dance floor is out."

She'd learned at an early age she had two left feet. Except under very specific circumstances like her parents' anniversary party when she danced with her dad and her sister's wedding when she'd danced with her brother, she stayed far away from dance floors. She'd been happy when Brett told her he never willingly ventured onto them either. Tonight though she'd be willing to make a trip on to it for a slow dance or two with Brett.

"Let's just walk around," she answered.

They gave the dance floor a wide berth and headed toward the picnic tables. "Is that a dunk tank over there?" She pointed toward an object near the center of the green. She'd only ever seen them in movies.

"Affirmative," Brett answered. "I wonder what kind of bet he lost to find himself in there."

They watched as the man sitting inside dropped down into the water and a cheer went up from the people standing around the tank. When the man came back up, he pushed his hair out of his eyes and climbed back up on the bench.

"It could be some type of fund-raiser." The school district in her town was always doing various fund-raisers.

Together they managed a few more steps before two young girls zipped in front of them, forcing them to either stop or crash into the energetic youngsters.

"Grace and Brianna, you both need to be more careful," an older woman called, following behind the girls.

The girls stopped and looked around. When one of the girls spotted Brett, she smiled and waved at him. "Brett, guess what?" She skipped over to them, her pigtails swinging back and forth. "Jessie had the babies. I'm a big sister."

This must be his neighbor's daughter.

The girl who'd spoken pointed at her companion. "This is my cousin Brianna."

"And I'm their grandmother." The older woman joined them. "Rose Ellsbury," she said, extending her hand first toward Jen. "But please call me Rose. You must be my son and daughter-in-law's new neighbors. I saw the lights on in the house when I drove by."

"Can we go, Grammy? Brianna and I want to get a donut before they're all gone."

"Yes, of course, give me one second," Rose said, looking at her two granddaughters and using a voice similar to the one Mom used when talking to Bella. "Welcome to town. I think you'll both love living here."

Rose and the girls walked away before either Brett or Jen could correct her. "Friendly little girl," Jen said as she watched

Grace and her cousin half skip and half run toward the tables filled with food.

HE'D VISITED a lot of places in his life, but he'd never seen anything quite like the events taking place around him. And although not something he'd want to attend every month, he could see himself making it to one next year. Brett waved back at Grace, who was now standing in line at a bounce house. Since first coming up to him and Jen, she'd passed by him twice and each time she'd waved in his direction.

"I think she likes you," Jen said.

"What?"

"Grace, your neighbor. I think she has a crush on you." She leaned into his side and whispered in his ear, "She's got good taste."

Brett looked at the girl standing in line with her cousin and then over at Jen. "She's what, seven, maybe eight years old? She's just friendly." Girls that young didn't have crushes.

Jen made a tsking sound. "You've got a lot to learn. I had my first crush in second grade. His name was Mr. Fellows, and he was my gym teacher. I was devastated when he married one of the third grade teachers at the end of the school year."

He tried to picture a seven-year-old Jen crying over her gym teacher. But he just couldn't do it. "If you say so."

Brett carried their drinks and looked around for a place to sit. The number of people on the common had doubled since they'd arrived. Rather than find an empty table, he spotted his friend Sean O'Brien. Some kind of strange contraption with tiny legs sticking out of it was attached to his chest. His wife sat next to him.

"There's someone I'd like you to meet," Brett said, before walking toward Sean's table.

Sean and his wife were in the middle of a conversation, but

when Brett stopped alongside the table they turned their attention toward him.

"Mia, Sean," Brett said, greeting the couple.

"Hey, glad to see you made it tonight," Sean said. "Have a seat."

"We had no other plans, so we decided to come over," Brett answered before looking at Jen. "Jen, this is Sean O'Brien and his wife, Mia."

Sean's wife needed no formal introduction. The woman had started starring in television shows and movies as a kid. Since meeting Sean though she'd taken a break from Hollywood and gone back to finish the college degree she'd started several years ago. He looked at the happy couple and tilted his head in Jen's direction. "I'd like you to meet my girlfriend, Jen."

The three of them exchanged greetings before Sean spoke again. "Jake's here tonight. He and Charlie came up for Ma's birthday. He's over getting some food."

"Sean's sister is married to my cousin," Brett explained to Jen. "Charlie's not here?"

The infant attached to his friend made a noise and a tiny pink-covered foot moved. Immediately Sean started to unbuckle the contraption holding his daughter in place. "She went to visit her friend at the hospital. Jessie had her babies late last night." Sean handed the little bundle to his wife and then he removed the carrier. "Jessie and Mack live next to you."

"I met them right after the storm. I saw the balloons outside their house this morning." Brett checked the area. Jake knew a lot more people in the political world than he did. Perhaps he'd heard of Phillip Young. The guy's name had been bugging him ever since his campaign manager told him his opponent had hired him. So far, he hadn't been able to place it, and he'd forgotten to ask his dad.

"And I ran into Grace tonight. She sounded happy when she

told me she's a big sister," he said as he continued scouting out the area.

Finally he saw Jake walking back toward their table with his son on his shoulders and an older woman walking alongside him. The woman had to be their nana's age and her mouth was going a mile a minute. Jake nodded and smiled as he listened.

"Have you met Mrs. Mitchell yet?" Mia asked as she repositioned her daughter against her shoulder.

Since Mia was looking in Jake's direction as well, Brett guessed the woman walking with his cousin was Mrs. Mitchell. "No."

"Looks like you're about to," Sean said moments before the older woman and Jake stopped at their table.

"I was going to call and see if you were around tonight," Jake said as he removed Garret from his shoulders and set him down on the bench. "Mrs. Mitchell, this is my cousin, Brett."

The older woman smiled warmly. "I saw your picture in the paper this week." Mrs. Mitchell walked closer and extended her hand toward Brett. "We're neighbors. I live on the other side of Jessie and Mack. If you ever need anything at all, please stop by. We take care of each other in this town." She patted his shoulder. "And just so you know, you have my vote in November. Ted Smith doesn't belong in any office."

"Thank you, ma'am. I appreciate it," Brett said.

Mrs. Mitchell touched his forearm. "None of that ma'am nonsense. Makes me feel old."

Brett heard Jake cough, and he wondered if it was his cousin's attempt to cover up a laugh. Mrs. Mitchell's comment was ridiculous after all, considering the woman had to be well over eighty years old.

"Call me Mrs. Mitchell like everyone else," she said.

"Will do."

After the older woman left, Jake took the empty seat between his son and Brett. "That woman knows everyone's business," Jake said.

"She always has," Sean said as he pulled a baby bottle out of the bag next to him.

"I think she's sweet," Mia said.

"Hey, I never said she wasn't. I like Mrs. Mitchell." Sean measured out baby formula before adding it to the water in the bottle. "But somehow she manages to keep tabs on everything going on in town. And she never forgets anything."

"Unlike some people at this table." Jake elbowed him hard in the side.

Brett immediately returned the gesture. "Jen, I hate to do this to you, especially when you'll have to meet more of my family tomorrow, but this annoying creature is my cousin Jake." As expected, the comment earned him another swift elbow to the side.

Jake leaned forward so he could see Jen. "I believe he meant to say amazing. My cousin's command of the English language has always been lacking. It's a bit embarrassing, really."

The corners of Jen's mouth twitched, and he waited for a smile to form. "Sorry, but I have to disagree. We've exchanged plenty of messages and they've all been well written. If Brett said annoying, it's what he meant." The smile she was trying to hold back finally took over.

Jake nodded. "You're going to get along well with my wife. For some reason, she never agrees with me either."

"That's because my sister is smart," Sean said as he stood. "I'll be right back."

"How old is she?" Jen asked, ignoring all the men at the table.

"Almost two months. Natalie was born in June."

While Mia and Jen discussed the baby, Brett turned his attention to his cousin, who at the moment was breaking a donut up into much smaller pieces for his son.

"Do you know a Phillip Young?" Brett asked.

Jake's hands stopped, and he looked over at him. "Why?" he asked, his tone suspicious. "He's not working on your campaign is he? Because if he is, get rid of him now."

"No. I hired Carl Filmore. But Young is running things for Ted Smith. His name sounds familiar. I thought you might know him."

Jake slid the paper plate toward Garrett before answering. "Sara dated him. They were together during part of Dad's campaign." His cousin no longer sounded suspicious. Instead he sounded pissed off. "Phillip is a slimy SOB. He plays dirty."

If his cousin Sara had dated the man, it explained why the name sounded familiar.

"Watch yourself around him. There isn't anything the man won't do to get the outcome he wants," Jake said.

He hadn't met all the men his cousin had dated before getting married, but the man Jake described didn't sound like someone Sara would've ever been attracted to. Or perhaps he didn't know his family members as well as he thought. "Will do. Thanks for the heads-up."

The scent of the fresh donuts and fried dough Sean set down reached Brett across the table. Neither of them had eaten before leaving his house. The scent of the grilling meat and various snacks sitting on the table now had his stomach loudly protesting its empty status. "That looks too good to pass up." He pointed toward the fried dough Sean passed to his wife. "Jen, do you want anything?"

"Maybe one of those donuts. They look amazing." She didn't look up from the baby she was holding.

"I'll be back."

"Hey what about me?" Jake asked. "Did you ever stop to think I might be hungry?"

"You've got two good feet. Use them."

Jake got up too. "I hope you know what kind of guy you've

gotten yourself involved with, Jen." He leaned closer to his son. "Garrett, stay with Uncle Sean. I'm going to get something for myself."

His cousin might want a snack—Jake had always been able to eat as much as him—but Brett knew it wasn't his only reason for accompanying him to the food tables. He had questions about Jen, because it was an unspoken rule that no one ever brought casual dates to family-only events like Allison's engagement party tomorrow.

Jake remained silent until they got several feet from the picnic table. "How long have you known Jen?"

Fair question. He'd attended their cousin Gray's wedding in June solo. Jake would assume they'd met since his move back to the area.

"Almost two years." Brett joined the line waiting for home-made donuts and fried dough.

"Then she's from Virginia? You should've brought her around when you came over."

Since Jake and his wife lived in Virginia, he'd made fairly regular visits to their house while he'd been stationed down there. He'd made all those visits alone.

"No. North Smithfield. She works in Providence, not far from Derek's office."

He should give his cousin all the details, but it was more fun letting him try to piece it together and then correcting Jake when he got it wrong. Brett watched Jake as he mulled over the information. He'd never told anyone about the letters he and Jen had exchanged.

Finally, Jake planted his hands on his hips. "I give up. How'd you meet? Is she a friend of Leah's?"

"No, so far she's only been unfortunate enough to meet you and Derek." He loved giving his family a hard time too much to resist.

"If she's spending time with you, she can't be too picky."

113

Jake, as well as the other male members of their family, always gave as good as he got. Brett couldn't imagine it any other way.

"During one of my deployments, Jen's scout troop sent us care packages. I got one with a letter from her. We started writing back and forth. Things progressed from there." Brett stepped forward as the line moved. "We met face-to-face for the first time a few days after I saw you in Connecticut."

"And you're bringing her to the engagement party. We both know what that means."

Yeah, Jen was important to him. He didn't need his cousin to point it out to him.

"There's only one Sherbrooke left now for you-know-who to chase after," Jake said as they reached the front of the line. "She'll be doubling up her efforts."

He hadn't seen or even thought about Richard Marshall's daughter in years, yet he knew that was whom his cousin was referring to. For longer than anyone could remember, Richard's youngest daughter, Tasha, had been trying to bag a male member of the Sherbrooke family. She'd even gone so far as to try to buy his cousin Derek at a bachelor auction the previous year. From what he'd heard, a little deception on his cousin's part had thwarted her plan.

"She doesn't stand a chance."

"You and I know that. I don't think Tasha does," Jake answered after giving Mrs. Mitchell his order.

Brett followed and ordered a donut as well as a piece of the fried dough. He couldn't remember the last time he'd had any, and with it in front of him, his sweet tooth made passing on it impossible. After accepting the red-hot treat he moved down the table and poured a generous helping of cinnamon and sugar over it while his cousin waited.

"Do you think your girlfriend is ready to meet everyone

tomorrow? Even Sara and Christopher are flying out for the party."

He'd expected it to be a smaller affair, considering how last-minute it'd been. If his cousin and her husband who lived in California were attending, it might not be as small as he'd thought. Not that it mattered to him. He wanted Jen to meet everyone who was important to him.

"I think the only ones who won't be there are Callie and Dylan. They went to visit Dylan's father in England," Jake said, confirming Brett's belief.

"She survived meeting you tonight. If she can do that, she'll be fine tomorrow."

"Nice. Real nice. For that I'm going to take you off my Christmas card list."

"Yeah, but your wife will put me back on, so I'm not worried."

BRETT FOLLOWED JEN INSIDE. They'd spent close to two hours at the block party. He'd even broken one of his personal rules and stepped on the dance floor. When Charlie, his cousin's wife, finally joined them, she somehow persuaded him to ask Jen to dance. He'd only done it because he expected she'd flat-out tell him no. If he'd asked while the DJ played a popular dance hit, he knew she would've too. Instead he'd asked just as the guy put on a slow sappy love ballad, the kind that usually had him changing the station. Jen had considered his question for less than a second before leading him to the temporary dance floor and slipping her arms around him.

He didn't regret their dance. It had given him a chance to hold her as close as he wanted despite the crowd. Perhaps dancing had some perks he'd overlooked in the past.

After the party, they along with Jake and his wife had gone

back to Sean and Mia's house. He wasn't sure how long Sean had owned the house, but he knew his friend had spent a lot of time restoring the old Queen Anne-style home to its former beauty.

"When my niece was born, I thought she was big. Your friend's daughter was like a giant compared to Bella at that age."

He'd thought Sean's daughter was tiny. In fact, when Sean's wife asked if he wanted to hold the baby, he'd declined, afraid he'd somehow hurt something so little. "Natalie is big?" He hadn't spent much time around infants, but if Jen considered Sean's daughter big, he didn't want to see one she considered small.

She headed toward the kitchen and the back door, Bo right at her feet. "Not big as in chubby, but she's long. When my niece was her age she was about twenty-three inches long, which is on the taller side. Sean and Mia's daughter was definitely longer than that." She opened the door and Bo darted outside. "But Sean is tall and Mia is taller than average, so it makes sense." Jen walked away from the door and back toward the living room. "After being stuck inside for so long, he'll be out there a while."

"My sister is going to flip when I tell her I got to meet not only Mia Troy but Prince Charming," Jen said, using the nickname the media had given his cousin Jake numerous years ago. "She used to have a huge crush on him. She couldn't see a magazine with his picture on the cover and not buy it."

Brett sat down next to her and put an arm over her shoulders. "If you ever want to get Jake annoyed, call him that. He hates it. Drives him up the wall."

"I'm surprised you don't use it all the time then. The two of you seem to love giving each other a hard time. It reminded me of the time we spent with your other cousin and his wife in Newport." She rested her hand on his leg. "Do you all act like that with each other?

116

"More or less," he answered as he slowly worked her hair free of its braid. "We spent a lot of time together growing up. Sometimes we act more like siblings than cousins." With her hair free, he ran his fingers through it. "You'll see what I mean tomorrow."

When he'd invited her along, he expected a handful of people to be there. Now that he knew better, he figured it was only fair to give her a heads-up. "Jake told me almost everyone will be on hand tomorrow. If you want to wait and meet my family members in smaller batches, I understand. Some might find meeting them all at once overwhelming."

Jen moved away from him, and her hair slipped from between his fingers. "I'm still up for going." She shrugged a shoulder. "But if you want to wait, I understand. This engagement party does sound like a major family event."

He hadn't intended to make her think he didn't want her there. Judging by her tone of voice, that was how she'd interpreted it. Time to do some damage control. "I want you there. I only wanted to give you fair warning. Being around my family can be enough to scare a battle-hardened general into retreating. And if you changed your mind about going, I'd skip it too."

"I never retreat."

"Neither do I." Brett pulled her in close and pressed his lips against hers. Jake's assessment earlier had been spot-on. He'd found the woman meant for him.

CHAPTER 9

THEY'D DRIVEN BACK to her house this morning in separate cars. During most of the ride home, she'd kept up a steady one-sided conversation with Bo, who sat in the passenger seat content to have his head halfway out the window. Despite all the reminders Brett's family members were just people who got up every day and showered like her, she couldn't shake the nervous jitters. The same jitters now had her looking at her reflection in the full-length mirror and thinking about changing her clothes. Again. She'd already put on and taken off three different outfits, not to mention the sundress she'd put on this morning at Brett's house.

She turned to see a different angle and wished there was someone besides Brett around to ask for a second opinion. He'd insisted she looked great in her first choice. Of course he also told her she looked great dressed in one of his T-shirts, so she didn't put much stock in his opinion.

"What do you think, Bo?" she asked the dog as he entered the room. He had been in the living room enjoying a treat. If he was here now, he'd finished it and was hoping for another one. Bo jumped on the bed and curled up on the sundress she'd worn home. "I guess you're telling me not to wear that one."

She gave the dog a scratch behind the ear and then picked up the lilac sundress she'd tried on before the outfit she wore now. Immediately, she put it back down.

That one might be better. She eyed the red floral dress on her pillow and reached for the zipper on her skirt. The knock on the partially open door stopped her from pulling it down.

"Can I come in?" Brett asked from the hallway.

She'd left him in the living room too. If he was looking for her, he must be getting antsy to leave. He'd seen her naked. She didn't see any reason to make him wait in the hall while she dressed. "Sure."

She waited until he came into the room before she picked up one of the dresses from the bed. "Do you think I should wear what I have on or this?" She held up the red floral dress.

"What was wrong with the one you had on when we got here?"

"Nothing. But I thought one of these outfits might be better." She held the dress up against her body. "So, which one should I go with?" She moved the dress away again so he could see what she had on.

His eyes went from the dress she held to the one Bo was napping on and then to the clothes she wore. "Whatever you're comfortable in. It's only my family, Jen. They won't care."

She wanted to make a great impression this afternoon. "Whatever you're comfortable in" wouldn't cut it today. "You're not very helpful." Jen turned back to the mirror. She'd put back on the first dress she'd tried. "Give me two more minutes, and I'll be ready."

Brett took the dress she held and tossed it back on the bed. It landed on Bo's head, but he didn't seem bothered in the least. He didn't so much as twitch an ear. "Trust me. You look amazing as is. No need to change. C'mon, let's go."

She'd driven through the Barrington area a few times and considered it one of the more beautiful towns in the state.

Located along the coast, it attracted many of the wealthier Rhode Island residents. The houses they'd passed so far reinforced the fact Barrington was one of the most affluent areas in Rhode Island.

Elegant and classic were the two words best suited to describe the home they approached as they drove through the open gate and down the driveway. Although larger than some of the mansions she'd passed during a Hollywood sightseeing tour, this mansion didn't look like it had been designed to catch people's attention like the ones she'd seen in California.

"It looks like some people are already here," she said. She checked out the other cars as he parked. She didn't know the make and model of them all, but many were more in line with what she'd originally expected Brett to drive.

Brett turned off the car. "I'll do my best to protect you from my cousins and siblings today. If one of them starts to annoy you too much, feel free to walk away or give them a smack on the back of the head. Especially my brother." He sounded serious, but the tiny smile poking through ruined the moment.

"Oh, knock it off. I've seen you with your cousins. You love your family."

He put his finger against his lips. "Ssh. Let's keep it our little secret." Dropping his hand, he leaned across the car and kissed her cheek. "In case my dad or one of my uncles is watching, will you please wait and let me open the door for you today? Dad will rip me a new one if catches me letting you open the car door for yourself."

With her hand on the door handle, she paused and considered his request. He'd insisted on opening doors for her at Turin and Pirate's Cove as well as whenever they got into his car. And once he'd complained when she'd gotten out of the car before he even opened his door. Until his statement, she hadn't realized it was such a big deal to him. "Are you serious?"

Brett nodded and there wasn't a hint of laughter in his

expression. "Dad's got views on how a gentleman should behave. Opening doors for women is on his list of things every gentleman must do. If they're together, you'll never see Mom open a door for herself. He along with my uncles drilled the entire list into me, my brother, and all my male cousins."

The list sounded old fashioned, but there were worse things to be in the world than old fashioned. If Brett considered it so important, she'd concede on certain occasions. "Since I don't want you getting in trouble and grounded, I'll let you do it today." She couldn't contain a chuckle as she envisioned Brett's dad scolding him. "But don't make a habit of it. When we're not around your family, I'll take care of it myself. Understood?"

"Affirmative."

While she waited for Brett to come around, she checked out the various license plates on the cars. Two were from Rhode Island, but there was also one from New Hampshire and another two from Virginia. Despite the short notice, it looked like plenty of family members had made it to this afternoon's engagement party.

When he opened the door, Jen accepted the hand he held out. "One of these days you'll have to tell me what other things are on your dad's list," she said.

"A conversation on that topic could take a while. Not to mention it'd be as boring as hell. Maybe one night if we have trouble falling asleep, I'll share it with you."

Brett rang the doorbell, and Jen waited for a uniformed employee to answer the door. Wealthy families hired people to handle those types of mundane tasks. At least in the movies they did. The bright smile the woman who answered the door gave Brett suggested she wasn't an employee but a family member.

"I was so happy when Mark said you might be coming today." The woman hugged Brett. "Everything was such short notice, and I know how busy you are with the campaign."

Wrapped in Brett's arms, the woman looked tiny. Before

releasing her, he kissed her cheek and then took Jen's hand. "Jen, I'd like you to meet Abby, Uncle Mark's wife." Brett didn't give Jen a chance to speak. "Abby, my girlfriend, Jen."

Twice now he'd referred to her as his girlfriend. Still, hearing the title attached to her sounded odd.

Abby turned her warm smile in Jen's direction and she couldn't help but return it. "Welcome. My husband mentioned Brett might be bringing a guest." Abby gave her a brief hug too. "I'm so glad you could make it as well. Please come in and make yourself at home."

They managed to make it through the door before the same little boy she'd seen at the block party zipped through the foyer running as fast as his little legs would carry him, which was rather fast considering the boy couldn't be much more than a year and a half old. Seconds later another boy who looked very close in age came running after him. Neither paused nor acknowledged the adults as they turned a corner, but their giggling could still be heard.

"If those two hellions are here, Jake and Trent are around too," Brett said, sounding amused.

Abby nodded. "When Garret and Kendrick get together, you never know what kind of mischief they might stir up. If they were a little older, I wouldn't be surprised to find Jake and Trent tied up in a closet somewhere."

"Sounds like both little guys are taking after their fathers," Brett said before glancing in Jen's direction. "The second blond streak who went through is my cousin Trent's son. Kendrick is a couple months younger than Jake's." He looked back at Abby again. "If they ever need help tying my cousins up, I'm there for them. I'll have to let them know that."

Abby flicked Brett's ear and shook her head. "Don't you dare, they'd go in search of some rope."

He'd addressed the woman by her first name rather than using the title aunt although she was married to his uncle. The way they joked with each other hinted at a good relationship though. If she thought of it later, she'd have to ask him why he didn't call her Aunt Abby. She'd never think to call any of her aunts by their given names. And if she'd ever tried as a child, Mom and Dad would've corrected her in a heartbeat.

"Don't worry, Mrs. Sherbrooke, I'll make sure he behaves while he's here today," Jen said, dismissing the other matter from her thoughts.

"Excellent, someone who can keep you in line, Brett." The older woman touched Jen's shoulder. "But please call me Abby." She glanced back toward Brett again. "Most of the family is out on the east lawn, but we are still waiting for a few people. I'm going to check on lunch, I'll be outside shortly." She walked away, leaving Brett and Jen alone.

"We can still retreat. No one but Abby knows we're here," Brett said.

"You survived meeting my family yesterday. I'll manage." If the rest of his family was as friendly as the few relatives she'd met so far, today would be a breeze.

"Who said I was worried about you? I was thinking about how much I'd rather be alone with you." He kissed her cheek then took her hand and started walking through the house. Like the exterior, the inside of the home could only be described as classic and elegant.

SHE TRIED TO ACT CALM, but little things kept giving her away— such as her sweaty palm. He knew his family though. They'd do their best to put her at ease and make her feel welcome. If they had any questions or concerns, they'd speak to him about them in private.

Brett led her down a hallway and out to the east lawn. When he and his cousins had been younger, they'd played hide-and-go-seek in this section of the estate. Back then a large maze of hedges, various flowering bushes, and fountains had occupied the space, making it a perfect place to hide. Following Aunt Donna's death, Uncle Mark had remarried and his second wife had wiped out the entire area. One of the first things Uncle Mark did once he divorced the woman was have a new garden planted. While not as elaborate as the maze that had been there, it was a nice reminder of Aunt Donna, a woman his uncle had never stopped loving. It was also a popular spot for the family to gather. During Brett's last visit the previous year, he'd noticed Abby had once again added to the area.

Today a large white tent had been set up just past the row of rosebushes. The sides of it were pulled open, and he could see the round tables inside. At the moment, no one was using the tent. Instead his various family members we seated on the padded patio furniture and benches situated inside the garden.

"Now this is a flower garden," Jen said softly as he pulled the French doors closed behind them.

He'd never cared much for flowers, but he knew she liked them. To someone who enjoyed gardening, this part of the estate as well as the greenhouse would be an absolute paradise. "Take your time and look around. We can check out the greenhouse too."

Across the garden, he saw his dad and mom exchange words. Then they both stood and started toward them.

"Maybe later. Your parents are headed this way," she answered as she took a step closer to him. "You look a lot like your mom. But you probably already know that."

It wasn't the first time someone had told him the same thing. He considered it a plus. His dad resembled his two older broth-ers. They all had the trademark Sherbrooke blue eyes and dirty-blond hair, although they all were sporting a fair amount of gray these days, especially Uncle Warren, the eldest of the bunch. Many of Brett's cousins had inherited those same features, and it made flying under the media's radar difficult and at times all-out impossible. He'd always had a much easier time of it thanks to the fact he'd inherited his looks from his mom's family. His younger brother hadn't been so lucky. Curt took after their dad, although his hair was a few shades darker. His younger sister was a nice mix of both parents.

Brett didn't know when he'd started doing it but whenever both his parents were around, he always greeted his mom first. So, when his parents reached them, he stepped forward and hugged her before even casting a glance toward Dad.

"I hoped to see you today," Mom said, returning his hug. "Your dad told me not to get my hopes up because you're busy with the campaign." She released him and looked at Jen before meeting his eyes again, her question quite obvious. Mom wanted to know who this was and why he'd never mentioned Jen before if she was important enough to bring to a family-only party.

He put an arm around Jen and looked at his parents. "You already know this, Jen, but these are my parents. Mom, Dad, my girlfriend, Jen."

His dad's eyebrow inched up the slightest amount. In fact, if he hadn't been watching for a reaction, Brett would've missed it. Dad was wondering why Brett hadn't mentioned Jen during any of their recent calls or meetings. He was also wondering how she might affect Brett's campaign. Mom gave him a look that said "we'll talk later" and then she smiled at Jen.

"It's wonderful to meet you," Mom said as she moved in to give Jen a hug. "I look forward to hearing how you and my son met. But first I'll introduce you to everyone."

Brett got the hint. Dad wanted a private word with him and he wouldn't wait. "Thanks, Mom." He squeezed Jen's hand. "Go ahead. I have a few campaign updates to discuss with Dad. I'll be right over."

He watched Mom lead Jen toward the rest of the family. He couldn't see her face, but he knew she'd be chatting away with Jen as if they'd always known each other. She was like that with everyone she came in contact with regardless of whether it was the barista making her latte or the governor's wife. When the two women reached the rest of the family, Brett turned his eyes back toward Dad and waited for his questions.

"I didn't expect you to arrive today with a date," Dad said. "How long have you known Jen?"

"Closing in on two years. I know her brother, Keith, too."

Both eyebrows went up this time. "I see. Does she realize the time constraints this campaign will put on you? Or how a win will affect your life?"

They hadn't sat down and actually discussed it, but she seemed to understand. And since they'd been seeing each other, she'd never made any demands on him. "Affirmative." He hated to lie but for now it was what Dad needed to hear.

Dad nodded slightly and looked toward where Jen stood with Mom. "You never mentioned her to your mom or me. Any particular reason?"

While Brett realized his father loved him, he didn't always understand the decisions he made. If it been up to him, Brett would've attended Harvard or Yale and then joined Sherbrooke Enterprises or perhaps the financial world like his younger brother had after college. He'd been quite vocal about Brett's decision to attend West Point and not follow the typical path of a Sherbrooke. Falling for a woman while exchanging letters and text messages would be one of those things Dad wouldn't understand. And if it hadn't happened to him, he wouldn't either.

"I just wasn't ready." It was a simple answer and one that wouldn't involve admitting that although they'd known each other a long time, they'd only met face-to-face this month.

Dad clapped him on the shoulder. "Well, if you brought her with you today, she must be important to you. I look forward to getting to know her better."

By the time they joined the rest of the group, Jen was already seated next to his cousin Allison and chatting away with the other women gathered. Since Allison was there, her new fiancé must be too, however at the moment he wasn't with the group. His cousins Jake and Trent weren't there either, although they couldn't be far since their wives were out here. Curt was there though, along with his girlfriend, Taylor. When he'd gone to pick up the key to Curt's house in Newport, he'd told his brother about Jen, so at least he wouldn't get any questions from him or Jake today. The rest of his cousins would corner him at some point before the day was out and grill him.

"I can't believe you've been back a few weeks and haven't stopped by or at least called us," Aunt Marilyn said when she spotted him.

Dad's only sister, Aunt Marilyn, had always been his favorite aunt, although he'd never tell anyone else that because he adored Aunt Elizabeth and had loved spending time with Aunt Donna before she passed away. Aunt Marilyn though had always been the most laid-back of the group. He didn't know how she'd turned out like that. All three of her brothers, as well as Brett's grandparents, were all so uptight and proper. Somehow Aunt Marilyn had managed to follow her own path.

"This campaign has taken over my life, Aunt Marilyn. I'll try to visit soon," he said as he mentally ran through his upcoming schedule. "I'm not sure when, but sometime in the next few weeks."

"Only if you have the time. Don't go out of your way to visit, but a phone call now and then would be wonderful," she said.

"That I can definitely do," Brett answered.

~

HE SPENT the next few hours catching up with his family and then enjoying a long, leisurely lunch. However, when the woman began discussing color schemes and floral arrangements best suited for a spring wedding, he along with the other male members of the family split. Now Brett, his cousins, and Rock, Allison's fiancé, were seated in the library enjoying drinks and conversations that didn't involve whether Allison's bridal bouquet should contain roses or not. The older male members of the family and Rock's father had hidden themselves in Uncle Mark's office until the debate over the best color for bridesmaid dresses ended. With so many women present and sharing their ideas, Brett knew all the men would be in hiding for a decent amount of time.

"Are you positive you want to join this family?" Brett asked. "There's still time to run. Once you say 'I do' you're stuck. There will be no turning back."

A United States Marine, Rock was stationed in Quantico, Virginia, and Brett had gotten to know his cousin's fiancé well. Since he already considered Rock part of the family, he had no qualms about giving the man a hard time like he would anyone else seated around them.

"It's already too late. If I tried to run away, Allison would track me down," Rock answered with a grim expression. An expression Brett knew was all an act. The guy adored Allison.

"Yeah, and if she didn't, I would. And don't forget it," Derek said. Although he and Allison were twins and only minutes apart, Derek had always played the role of protective older brother. It drove Allison crazy. Brett figured it was part of why Derek insisted on doing it.

"Allison doesn't need our help, and we all know it," Trent said before looking at Rock, who was not only his sister's fiancé but also his wife's older brother. "But we'd still step in if the need ever came up. Which we know it won't."

Sometimes he felt sorry for Allison. His cousin had four brothers and all of them, even Alec who was younger than Allison, had always kept a watchful eye over her. Especially after their mom passed away. "Welcome to the family, Rock." Brett raised his glass in a toast before he took a sip.

"So, when's your trip to the altar going to be?" Trent asked, finally giving Allison's fiancé a break and looking at Brett.

"Yeah, we're going to have to add your name to the pool," Jake said.

"My money is still on Scott," Derek said, referring to their cousin who hadn't made it to the party. "He and Paige will get married first." Derek smiled as if he knew something everyone else didn't.

Brett looked across to his brother. "I'm guessing they already added your name, little brother."

Curt only shrugged. "First I'm hearing of this," he said, and looked at their smiling cousin. "What do you know the rest of us don't, Derek?"

"Scott planned to propose this weekend. Unless Paige realized she could do better, they should be engaged as of now," Derek answered.

"Looks like you two are way behind in the running," Trent said.

Jake put his glass down on a side table. "I don't know, Trent. They've both introduced their girlfriends to the family. They might not be as far behind Scott in the race to the altar as you think."

Trent seemed to consider Jake's words, and Brett waited to hear what words of wisdom he'd spit out next. Trent didn't keep him waiting long.

"Excellent point, Jake. I believe you're right. With all these weddings coming up, maybe I should buy another tuxedo in case they plan back-to-back ceremonies." Trent looked over at Alec, his youngest brother and the only single man in the room. "Maybe you can get in on this too. We can have one large wedding and save everyone a lot of time."

"Allison would never go for it. And for now I'm happy being

single," Alec said. "I'll leave the serious relationship stuff to you old guys."

Brett had been happy single too. Over the past couple weeks though, he'd realized what he'd been missing by being alone. And he had no plans to give up what he'd found.

CHAPTER 10

"I wish they'd find something else to talk about," Eden said.

Jen looked away from her computer screen and at her coworker. Before Jen's promotion and move to her own office, she'd sat in the cubicle next to Eden's. Back then it'd been common for them to chat during the day. Despite Jen's move to a real office with four walls and a door, they still visited with each other. At the moment, Eden stood at Jen's open door, a paper coffee cup from Ambrosia in her hand.

"Who would stop talking about what?" She'd been working on the same project all day, and a short conversation with Eden would be a nice break for both her brain and eyes.

Her coworker walked inside and sat down at one of the chairs near the desk. "The silly special election in Massachusetts. No matter what news site I check, there's a story about it. I don't live in Massachusetts and don't care who wins. There must be something else important the reporters can find to write about."

Jen might not live in Massachusetts, but she had strong feelings about the upcoming vote. On one hand, she wanted Brett to win. She knew how important it was to him. At the same time,

131

she knew a win would also mean he'd relocate to DC for at least part of the year. She didn't know how such a move might affect them. They hadn't discussed it, but if he won, he might end their new relationship. Even if he didn't, distance could put a strain on even time-tested relationships. With theirs being so new, the stress might be too much. When she considered that, she hoped Brett lost to Ted Smith in the primary. Unfortunately, those thoughts always kicked her guilt into action, making her feel like the worst girlfriend alive.

"And it's not just on the news and all over the internet. Last night I saw commercials for all the candidates multiple times while I was watching television. Seriously, if you have to show so many, put them on Massachusetts stations," Eden said.

She'd stopped watching regular television a long time ago because of all the commercials. Now she either set her DVR to record her favorite shows, allowing her to fast-forward through the commercials, or she watched shows on demand. Perhaps her friend should consider doing the same thing.

"New England's a small area. People often watch stations from other states. I'm not surprised they're all playing the same commercials," Jen said.

Eden pushed her eyeglasses on top of her head. "The media is only doing it because a Sherbrooke is running. If anyone else were going against Ted Smith, the coverage would be much less. And if after the primary it ends up being Ted Smith against, say, Gina Hammond, they'll hardly report anything anymore."

Jen didn't completely agree with her friend's assessment. This particular election was perhaps more important than most since it could change the balance of power in the Senate. So while Brett's involvement might be increasing the coverage slightly, there was a lot at stake. Even if he didn't win the primary, the media would stay focused on the election until the end.

"At least it won't last too much longer. The primary is on

November 7 and then the election will be December 19." Both dates were etched into her mind.

"Yeah, but then it'll all be replaced with stuff about the presidential primary and that election. I guess I better get used to it. Maybe some new big Hollywood scandal will break and distract the media from the election for a bit, giving us all break from politics."

"Do what I do. Record your favorite shows, then you can watch them when you want and skip over the commercials," Jen said.

"Sometimes I do, but often I hate waiting. And my boyfriend and I never record a football or baseball game. It's too easy to overhear people talking about it before we get a chance to watch it. Last night during the baseball game, every single break featured a political ad. Most were for either Ted Smith or Vince Reed, but even the third-party candidates got some air time."

The phone on Jen's desk rang, temporarily halting their conversation. The extension number displayed on the screen indicated the call was from the office receptionist and not an outside line. "Hello," she said. She didn't have any scheduled meetings for this afternoon and her clients usually called her line directly rather than go through Willow.

"Jennifer, you have a visitor here to see you," Willow, the receptionist, said.

Clients came to see her when they had appointments, but no one else. If her sister or mom did come to the city, they always met somewhere. They never unexpectedly showed up at the office. Actually, Jen didn't think either had ever stepped foot in the building. If one of them was there now, something terrible must have occurred. Jen ran her tongue over her bottom lip before she asked her next question. "Who is it?"

"Brett Sherbrooke."

Jen picked up on the excitement and the curiosity in the receptionist's voice.

"I don't see his name on your schedule. Should I show him to your office?" Willow asked.

They hadn't seen each other as much as she would've liked since his cousin's engagement party, but they'd talked on the phone on the days they couldn't get together. During those conversations, he always shared his upcoming schedule. She knew today he'd had an event in Seekonk. When they talked yesterday, he hadn't mentioned stopping in to see her afterward. "Uh, sure, Willow. That's fine. Thank you."

"Is something wrong?" Eden asked when Jen put down the phone receiver.

Jen shook her head and saved the document she was working on. Then she closed the file folder she had open on her desk. "No. There's just someone here to see me."

Outside of their families and the few people they'd talked to at the North Salem block party, no one knew of their involvement. She wasn't opposed to other people learning, but she wasn't sure how she felt about some of the first people being her coworkers. While she got along with all of them, there was only a handful such as Eden she actually considered a friend. She'd rather not provide the office with this week's water cooler gossip, and that was sure to happen if people saw Brett walk into her office.

Eden slipped her eyeglasses back on and picked up her paper coffee cup. "I was hoping to pass enough time so I didn't have to do any more work today. Oh well, I guess I'll have to spend a few more minutes at my desk." She came to her feet. "I'll see you tomorrow. Have a nice night."

She liked Eden as a person, but as an employee was another story. Her friend had a tendency to procrastinate and waste time, which was why she'd been passed over for so many promotions despite the number of years she'd worked at the firm.

"See you tomorrow." Jen watched Eden step out of the office, and then she turned her attention back to her desk. She didn't want anything left out with a client's personal information on display. While her work wasn't top secret or anything, she believed the firm's clients would want their privacy. She knew she would.

"You'll never guess who's here." Eden's excited voice announced she'd reentered Jen's office. "Brett Sherbrooke. Willow is bringing him back to see someone," she said, not giving Jen a chance to speak. "We were just talking about him. I can't believe he's here. I wonder who he is meeting with? I bet he's here to see Leovanni."

Leovanni Pike was the firm's president, and if Jen didn't know the truth, she would've made the same assumption. Should she tell Eden the truth or let her be surprised when Willow and Brett stopped at her office? "He's not meeting with Leovanni," she said.

Eden looked toward her, and Jen knew the second Eden realized whose office Willow and Brett were headed for. "That's right. Willow called because you have a visitor. He's your visitor. Why is Brett Sherbrooke here to see you?" she asked in a low whisper before glancing back over her shoulder. "Never mind. They're almost here. You can tell me later." She bolted from the office and down the hall.

She'd seen him in various types of clothing, but until now she'd hadn't seen him in a suit. Standing there dressed in a perfectly tailored three-piece charcoal-gray suit, he looked every inch the polished Washington politician. *It's only Brett.*

"This is Jennifer's office." Willow stopped just outside the doorway and gestured toward the open door.

Brett smiled. It was the same smile he'd used for the photographer who had taken the picture that graced the landing page of the *Providence Gazette*'s website this morning. A similar picture had been attached to an article in the *Boston Times* earlier in the week. Jen had dubbed the expression his campaign smile. While it looked natural, it wasn't the same smile he shared with her or his family.

"Thank you for your help. I appreciate it," he said, earning him a smile from Willow before she walked away.

When he turned his full attention Jen's way, he gave her a true smile and her thoughts immediately went to their good-night kiss Sunday night. It was closing in on five thirty, so most people would be leaving for the night. Perhaps if she closed the door, she could give him a similar one now.

"I should've called first." Brett moved the knot of his dark blue tie down a smidge. "I hope you don't mind that I stopped in, but I missed you, and Providence was on my way home."

I missed you. He'd said the same three words during each of their conversations this week. The sentiment was returned 100 percent.

"Of course not. I'm glad you did. I've missed you too." Jen walked around her desk and closed the door, intending to give him at least a hug. Brett beat her to it. The moment the door clicked, he stepped close and pulled her into his arms.

"The whole drive here I had one thing on my mind," he said.

"A sweet snack?" she asked. The man had a sweet tooth that surpassed a five-year-old child's.

He lowered his head toward hers, stopping when their lips were mere inches apart. "Not exactly." He brushed his lips across hers, a light caress she somehow felt from the tips of her toes to the top of her head.

"That's what you were thinking about?"

"As well as a few other things we unfortunately can't do in your office." Brett winked at her.

For a moment, she considered the likelihood of anyone knocking on the office door. Almost as quickly she dismissed the idea. No matter how much you wanted to, there were some things you didn't do in your office. "I can leave soon. Do you want to come to my house? I can cook us dinner." *And we can do anything else we want.*

He touched his forehead against hers. "I'd like nothing more."

"I hear a 'but' in your voice," she said.

"But I've got a meeting with Carl and my team tonight." He sounded as disappointed as she felt. "Between work and all the other events this week, it was the only time I could squeeze in a meeting with them all."

Standing so close, she could see the dark circles under his eyes. It was clear he'd been burning the candle at both ends all week. She still believed he should take a leave of absence from work. She'd suggested it twice now, and he'd insisted it wasn't necessary. As much as she wanted to, she wouldn't suggest it again. Jen hoped either someone on his campaign team or a family member would, though. He couldn't keep up his current schedule forever and not burn himself out.

"Can I get a rain check?" he asked before glancing at his wristwatch.

Jen checked the time too. She could pack up and head home. "Anytime."

"Outstanding." He slid his tie down another fraction of an inch. "If I have any hope of making it to my meeting on time, I've got to go. Can you leave now? I parked in your parking garage, so if you can leave we can walk over together."

"Let me grab my things." It wouldn't take long to get from her office building to the parking garage, but she'd take what time she could get with him.

It wasn't a surprise that most of the employees were gone as they walked through the office. With summer approaching its unofficial end, Labor Day weekend, everyone wanted to squeeze in what little time was left before children went back to school and the days became cooler. Since so many people had already left for the night and wouldn't see her and Brett leaving together, Jen hoped the gossip would be kept to a minimum tomorrow.

Downstairs Brett pushed open the door, and hot, humid air hit Jen head-on. She hadn't left the building all day, and the high temperature now was a big change from this morning. Behind her, Brett continued to hold the door as two other women exited after them. He didn't show it, but the poor man must be dying in his suit and tie.

"How long do you think your meeting will last?" she asked once they started down the sidewalk.

"No idea. Hopefully not too long. I've got an early morning tomorrow."

Although he seemed oblivious to the glances other people on the sidewalk sent their way, she wasn't. "Afterward, if you want to talk, call me." Unlike her sister, she'd never been one to go to bed early.

They entered the parking garage, and she went straight toward the stairwell. She found the elevators to be slow and avoided them. Jen figured by doing so she always got in a little exercise, and some days the trip up and down the stairs was the only exercise she managed.

"If it's not too late, I will. But I don't want to keep you up tonight." His hand landed on her lower back. "Tomorrow night is another story." His breath was a soft caress against her ear. "Should I come to your house or do you want to come to mine?"

His various campaign obligations had him driving all over the state. She couldn't help him with any of that, but she could make his life a little simpler and drive to North Salem tomorrow night. "I can come up after work." She stopped next to her car and opened the door. "Or later if you won't be home then. Whatever works for you." She tossed her bags in the car.

Brett eliminated the space between them, his chest coming in contact with her breasts. "Come right after work. By the time you get there, I should be home." His hands cupped her face, and

THE BILLIONAIRE'S HOMECOMING

he kissed her. "Pack enough for a few days." He kissed her again, this one lasting longer. "And bring along Bo so you can spend the weekend." He took her mouth again, his tongue darting inside to touch hers.

The sounds and smells around her disappeared into the background as she gave herself over to Brett's skilled mouth. Every pass of his lips over hers sent another ripple of sensual excitement through her body. Somehow each one managed to be more intense than the one before it.

"I wish you didn't have your meeting tonight," she said when he finally pulled away.

He kissed the erratic pulse in her neck. "Believe me, I do too." He kissed the spot again. "I promise I'll make it up to you this weekend."

Hoping to get her breathing back to normal, she took in a slow, deep breath and then blew it out. "I should have you put that in writing in case you change your mind."

The hands he'd moved around her waist while kissing her came back to her face. "Any promise I make to you, I'll keep."

PINCHING the bridge of his nose, Brett watched Jen back out of her parking spot. He was used to putting in long hours, but for some reason, the last couple weeks were taking a toll on him. He chalked it up to the fact the stress he was under now was much different than what he'd grown accustomed too.

Before Jen started for the exit, she smiled and waved at him. Only after she was on her way did Brett walk further down the garage to his car. A sound to his left caught his attention, and he watched another person back out of a parking spot. In fact, all around him people were getting ready to leave the city for the night.

Idiot. He gave himself a mental smack to the back of the head. They'd been in a very public parking garage. Anyone could've seen them kissing near her car. While they hadn't been doing anything inappropriate, a potential United States Senator shouldn't be seen making out in a downtown parking garage. He needed to be more careful. Right now, his opponents had nothing scandalous to use against him. He, along with his dad and Carl, wanted it to stay that way.

Brett rubbed the spot over his right eye and got behind the wheel. He kept a bottle of ibuprofen in the glove box. After starting the engine, he grabbed the bottle, popped three pills in his mouth, and swallowed. Hopefully, they'd take the edge off his headache, allowing him to make it through his upcoming meeting. Afterward he'd grab a few hours of sleep before heading back into Boston so he could put in a couple hours at Homeland Security before driving to Westborough for a luncheon at the senior center there.

From the moment he got on Interstate 95 in Providence, the traffic remained stop and go. It didn't let up as he crossed the state line and continued north toward Boston. Somehow though, he managed to reach the garage near Carl's office with ten minutes to spare, even after stopping along the way for a much-needed extra-large coffee. Thankfully, between the caffeine and the three ibuprofens he'd taken, it no longer felt as if his head might explode right on the sidewalk, ending his political aspirations.

"Brett, you look terrible," Dad said when he saw him.

He'd invited Dad to today's meeting. His father had his share of political experience, and Brett valued his opinion just as much as that of the people he'd hired to work on the campaign. Tonight, Brett had pulled into the parking garage just as his dad was getting out of his car.

"Are you feeling okay tonight?" Dad asked.

"Just a little tired. It's been a busy week," Brett answered. "Nothing some sleep won't take care of."

"So I've heard. But it's paying off. The polls still have you ahead of Smith by a wide margin."

He'd gotten the newest poll updates from Carl earlier today. While pleased with the data, he knew the battle wasn't over yet. A man like Ted Smith wouldn't go down without a damn good fight.

Dad reached the building entrance first and pulled open the door. "I didn't get a chance to speak with you before you left the engagement party or since."

Other than the brief conversation when they first arrived, Brett hadn't had a moment alone with his dad. Instead he'd spent much of the afternoon with Jen by his side and his family around him. For the hour or so when Jen had been busy with his female relations, he'd hung out with his brother and cousins. But if Dad had really needed or wanted to speak privately with him again, the man would've found an opportunity to pull him aside.

"Your mom and I both liked Jen. She seemed comfortable with the family too."

He'd noticed that by the time they'd left his uncle's house, she was acting as if she'd known his family all her life.

"Next time you have some free time, bring her over. We'd like to spend more time with the two of you." They stepped into the elevator and Dad pressed the button for Carl's floor. "Maybe Curt and Taylor can join us."

It sounded like Dad had already accepted Taylor into the family fold—not that his younger brother would end his relationship with Taylor if their dad didn't like her.

"I think you and your brother have both found women who'll fit nicely into the family. Your mom agrees with me."

When it came to whom he dated, Brett didn't need his parents' approval. However, the fact they both liked Jen and we're prepared to welcome her to the family pleased him.

The light indicating they'd reached the tenth floor lit up, and the doors opened. "Will do. But it might not be for several weeks." He didn't have a lot of free time. What little he had, he'd rather spend with Jen, not Jen, his parents, and brother.

They approached the reception area and Brett checked in with the office receptionist.

"Yes, I've seen your upcoming schedule. I think you should plan to take Jen to some of the events," Dad said while they waited to go into Carl's office.

"Why?"

"Voters view a candidate in a stable relationship more favorably than one who's single. While you have a decent lead over Ted, there's no reason not do everything you can to increase and maintain it. Trust me. Showing up with Jen will go a long way with the voters."

Down the hallway, Carl's office door opened and his assistant started toward the reception area. Before she reached them and overheard their conversation, Brett said, "I'm not sure how Jen would feel about coming."

"If you win this election, she'll have to get used to such events. The sooner you help her get used to them, the better."

They hadn't talked about how his life would change if he won and what it would mean to their relationship. It wasn't that he was avoiding it. It simply hadn't occurred to him, and she never brought up the topic. Brett didn't know if his dad was right about voters liking candidates in stable relationships more or not, but he was right about Jen having to attending various social events if he won. He'd have to prepare her for the possibility.

"I'll talk to her about coming to a few. I'm seeing her this weekend," Brett said.

Carl's assistant, Dee, reached them and smiled. "Good evening, gentlemen. Mr. Filmore is ready for you."

Later he'd review his upcoming schedule and see which public events Jen might be interested in. Right now, he'd concentrate on getting through this meeting despite the sudden renewed pounding in his head.

CHAPTER 11

Phillip reviewed the newest data. Despite all the baby kissing and handshaking Ted had done over the past couple of weeks, his numbers were not moving. They'd already spent a small fortune on television commercials and billboard ads. He had teams of Smith supporters out knocking on doors and putting up signs in every town and city across the Bay state. None of those efforts were paying off either. Like Phillip had feared it would, Ted's ultimate successes hinged on his plan to uncover something they could use against the golden boy, Brett Sherbrooke. And when Ted arrived in a few minutes, he'd want an update on Phillip's progress.

Up until several hours ago, he had feared they'd hit a brick wall on that front. It seemed everyone known to associate with Brett had just as disgustingly clean a background as he did. They couldn't even find a jilted woman or one-night stand in the man's past they could exploit to their own end. The man was like a super Boy Scout.

Today's edition of the *Boston Times* had given him a tiny hint of hope though.

A knock on his office door had him looking up from his computer screen.

"Mr. Smith is here to see you," his secretary said, poking her head inside the room.

"Send him in." Phillip finished typing the web address in and waited for the *Star Report*'s website to pop up. He never checked the site out. It contained only celebrity news and gossip, none of which he concerned himself with. Hollywood actors and reality stars didn't put money in his bank accounts. Politicians did. However, tonight he hoped to find something he could to use to his client's advantage. Sherbrooke might not be a movie star, but the media treated his family like celebrities. Hopefully, the national media was capitalizing on the same story the *Boston Times,* the *Worcester Daily News,* and the *Providence Gazette* had put out there today.

"Good to see you again, Phillip." Ted walked inside the room, his full swagger back in place. The momentary defeat Phillip had witnessed during their last private meeting at Ted's house was gone and thankfully it hadn't made a repeat appearance since. Phillip hoped it stayed that way until after the election. Once Ted was in Washington, he didn't care what happened to him or how he portrayed himself.

"Help yourself to a drink if you want before we begin." Phillip pointed toward the well-stocked wet bar across the room. Today's meeting would only be the two of them. The rest of the campaign staff didn't even know it was taking place. So if they decided to be more casual than usual, no one would know or care.

While Ted poured himself something, Phillip turned his attention to the popular magazine's website landing page. What he saw brought an immediate smile.

Ted set a drink down near Phillip's keyboard and sat across from him. "I reviewed the latest numbers," he said as he raised his glass toward his lips. "They haven't budged, and we're running out of time."

Phillip was aware of exactly how much time they had left. He didn't need Ted to remind him.

"Have you found anything we can use against Sherbrooke? No one can be as perfect as he seems," Ted said with disgust.

When it came to most people, Phillip would agree. Much to his annoyance, Brett Sherbrooke did seem above reproach. "I'm not sure. I was about to give up on that angle and focus on another. A new development came up recently."

A look of satisfaction crossed Ted's face. "Excellent. I had my doubts you'd find anything on him. The whole family acts like they're better than the rest of the world. Regardless of the outcome of this election, I'd be happy to see a member brought down a peg or two."

As much as he shared Ted's sentiments, he needed to set the record straight before Ted got too excited. "My contacts haven't uncovered anything useful on him." Phillip swiveled his chair and picked up the top newspaper on the back credenza. "Did you see this today?"

He passed a copy of the *Boston Times,* open to the society section, across the desk. A black-and-white photo of Brett Sherbrooke kissing a woman in a parking garage occupied a large portion of the page. A smaller one of them holding hands and walking down a sidewalk was also there, along with a short article by a reporter he wasn't familiar with.

"Similar pictures showed up in at least two other papers this morning." Phillip turned the computer screen so Ted could see the *Star Report*'s website and the almost identical picture featured there. "The *Star Report* picked up on the story too."

Ted studied the picture in the newspaper and then set it aside. "No, I haven't seen these. This morning was move-in day for my oldest son at Deerfield Academy. I promised him I'd be there. I went straight from there to my engagement at the VFW in

Grafton." His eyes moved across the computer screen. "Who is she?"

"The article says her name is Jennifer Wallace, and she works in Providence." The article hadn't given him anything useful except her name. He'd started with less information though. If she had any skeletons in her closet, he'd find them.

"What do we know about her?" Ted asked.

Phillip looked at the picture again. None of his contacts had uncovered Brett was in a romantic relationship. These pictures told a different story. He was involved with someone. Either it was a recent development or Sherbrooke had a reason for keeping it under the rug.

"Nothing useful yet. But my people are on it." Soon he'd know everything from when her birthday was to her favorite place to shop. "If she's got any secrets, we'll know about them. Don't worry. My best people are on it."

Ted's expression grew grim. "I won't get my hopes up. Judging by what we know of Sherbrooke, he wouldn't get himself involved with a woman who has something to hide." He tapped the newspaper on the desk. "Uncover what you can. But I don't want you wasting all my money on this. Your people have two weeks. After that we're ditching this strategy altogether."

His contacts were good. Two weeks should be more than enough time for them to uncover some useful dirt, assuming there was some out there.

"In the meantime, I want to revisit my upcoming events. Make sure the topic is given ample time at our meeting."

Bright and early Wednesday they had a strategy meeting with Ted's entire inner circle. Following it the former lieutenant governor had a town hall forum at one of the state's community colleges. "I'll make certain we address it," Phillip said.

CHAPTER 12

"MISS WALLACE, this is Daniella Nault with the *Star Report*," the caller said after Jen answered the phone.

Not another one. Didn't these reporters have better things to do with their days than call her? Since the pictures of her and Brett had shown up Monday, she'd been getting a constant string of phone calls and e-mails from various reporters. If being a celebrity was anything like this, she had a new appreciation for the men and women in Hollywood.

"I hope I'm not catching you at an inconvenient time," the reporter said.

In Jen's opinion, there was no convenient time for this woman or any of her colleagues to call. "Actually, I'm expecting guests." Normally, she didn't think of her sister and niece as guests, but if it helped get her out of this conversation without appearing like a rude witch, she'd use their upcoming visit.

"I understand and won't keep you long. I was hoping to set up a time for an exclusive interview with you. Ideally it would be in the next couple days so it can make the next edition of the *Star Report*. If that's not possible, I totally understand, and we can schedule it for a time more convenient for you. But I would require you not give any other interviews in the meantime."

The easiest thing would be to end the call and hope the reporter didn't call back. Unfortunately, the easiest thing would also be rude. As a rule, unless left with no other choice, she remained polite no matter the situation or person she faced. The constant calls and surprise visits by reporters all week were making it difficult to follow her personal rule.

"Ms. Nault, I have been contacted by a handful of other publications." Jen prepared to give the same speech she'd given to the last three reporters who'd called from major magazines.

"This isn't the nineteenth century," the reporter said with a little laugh. "Call me Daniella."

If the reporter thought being on a first-name basis would change anything, she was about to be disappointed. "Daniella, I know it's not the answer you were hoping for today, but I have no plans to do interviews with anyone. I'm sorry." She wasn't, but it seemed like the polite thing to say.

The first three publications had offered her a not-so-tiny sum of money to sit down and give them an interview they could get out to their readers before any of their competitors. The *Star Report* would most likely do the same. No matter what dollar amount the media giant presented her with, she'd refuse it.

"I truly understand your desire to protect your relationship, Jennifer. Really, I do, and in your shoes, I'd have my reservations as well."

Well, this is a different approach. The other reporters had become argumentative when she refused. "Thank you."

"But I still must ask you to reconsider. Many consider the Sherbrooke family American Royalty. People care about them and want glimpses into both their private and public lives."

Jen didn't disagree with the reporter's comments. People did love to read about the Sherbrookes. When it came to her and

Brett's relationship, she didn't care about what the public wanted.

"And people across the country are especially intrigued with Brett Sherbrooke right now. He's spent much of his life in the military and outside the public spotlight. Then suddenly he's running for a seat in the United States Senate with you by his side," Daniella said. "Readers want to know all they can about him and you."

The woman was good, Jen would give her that much. Not once during their conversation had she lost the friendly tone in her voice or given any hint at the frustration she was probably feeling because Jen refused to fall into line.

"I have River Michaels, the magazine's executive editor, here with me, Jennifer. Before you refuse again, he'd like to discuss compensation with you."

"Really, that won't—"

"Thank you for taking our call this afternoon," a male voice said, cutting off the rest of Jen's sentence. "As Daniella explained, we'd love to do an interview with you. Naturally, we'll compensate you for your time."

The executive editor rattled off a figure roughly five times what Jen made in a year, and she almost dropped the cell phone. The other publications had presented her with large dollar amounts too, but nowhere close to what the *Star Report* was willing to pay her.

When the doorbell rang, Jen started for the door. Before opening it, she peeked out a front window. She'd opened the door once earlier this week without checking because she thought it was Brett. Instead of finding him, she found a photographer and reporter from the *Providence Gazette* waiting on the other side. It had taken at least ten minutes to get rid of them.

"I'm sorry, Mr. Michaels." Jen opened the door and let her sister and niece inside. "My answer is still no."

"I'll give you my direct line and my e-mail address as well

as Daniella's information. If you change your mind at any time, please consider contacting us first."

The man rattled off the information, but Jen didn't even search for a piece of paper to write it on. No amount of time or money would change her mind on this one.

"Hi Auntie Jen," Bella said when Jen put the cell phone down. "Where's Bo?"

"In the backyard."

Bella left without a backward glance.

"You look frazzled," Kristen said once her daughter was out of hearing. "Is the media still bothering you?"

Jen nodded and flopped down onto the sofa. "Yep. That call was from a reporter at the *Star Report*."

"I love that magazine. It's the only one I read every week anymore, and it has great crossword puzzles."

"It might be your favorite, but I don't need them doing an article on me. You don't even want to know how much they were willing to pay me for an exclusive interview."

Kristen nodded. "You're probably right." They'd had a similar conversation after the first three magazines called offering money in exchange for a sit-down meeting. While Kristen understood why Jen turned them down, she'd admitted the payday associated with an interview would be hard to pass up.

"I'm not trying to sound like a bitch or anything, but what did you expect? You're dating a member of the Sherbrooke family. The media circles them like flies circle a pile of poop."

Her sister made a good point, but she could've done without Kristen's gross comparison. "I guess I didn't think about it at all. Until he entered the election, I don't remember ever seeing him on magazine covers like his cousins, so it never crossed my mind the media would want all the details about our relationship." Friends, family, and maybe coworkers, sure, but not the entire world.

"Unless you plan on ending your relationship soon, I think you better get used to it, sis."

She'd already reached the same conclusion. Unfortunately, she wasn't sure how to get used to random people asking for interviews or snapping pictures of her. "Trust me, I know."

"Did you ever find out who took the pictures in the garage?" Kristen asked.

"Nope." She'd called the *Providence Gazette* and asked. They'd refused to give her the information. She'd gotten similar responses from the *Boston Times* and *Worcester Daily News*. When she got nowhere, Brett offered to call and inquire. While she appreciated the gesture, she'd flat-out told him no. She didn't want him doing anything that could negatively impact his senate run. Especially since in the end, it didn't really matter who had snapped the pictures and sent them in. The damage was done.

"I still say it must be someone you work with. Everyone in your office uses the same parking garage, and they know you. The newspapers would've had to get your name to run with the story from whoever sent in the photos."

She'd reached a similar conclusion. "I can't question everyone I work with." If she could, she would've already done it.

"You didn't notice anyone around?"

Really, it was one of the dumbest questions she'd been asked in a long time. "Uh, I was a little preoccupied when the picture was taken."

"Good point." Kristen picked a loose thread off her shorts. "So what's on the agenda for this weekend?"

"Tomorrow we're going to a fund-raising event in Boston. I don't know much about it except it's black tie and being held at the Harbor House. I shouldn't be home too late on Sunday. Brett is meeting with several representatives from a conservation group Sunday afternoon."

"The Harbor House. Wow, I've read about the place. Mia Troy had her wedding reception there. You'll have to tell me all about it," Kristen said. A huge fan of the actress, Kristen had followed every detail printed about Mia's engagement and wedding. "The later you come by on Sunday, the happier Bella will be anyway. All week she's talked about having Bo at our house." Kristen paused and checked the doorway leading into the kitchen. "If Bella does another great job taking care of Bo this weekend, Dan's agreed to let her get a dog this fall. We haven't told her yet. We're waiting to see how it goes first."

There wasn't a doubt in Jen's mind her niece would do a wonderful job again. "I hope you're both prepared for a permanent four-legged friend of your own."

Her sister smiled. "I told Dan the same thing."

BRETT KEPT his sunglasses on as he opened the door into his house. It looked like the twenty-hour days had finally caught up to him. The nausea had started while still on the highway. At first he'd chalked it up to the fast-food burgers he'd grabbed at a rest stop on the Pike. When the aura started, he knew his upset stomach had nothing to do with food.

Crossing the kitchen, he focused on getting to somewhere he could lie down. When he reached the living room, he paused long enough to close all the blinds, blocking out as much sunlight as possible. Without even removing his tie or shoes, he hit the sofa and closed his eyes.

Someone bashed a mallet against a gong, and Brett forced his eyes open. He had no idea of how long he'd been lying there or what time it was. There was no light in the room to help him gauge it either. He did know he was on the sofa in his living room and he still wore his shoes. The mallet-wielding jerk beat their gong again, and he groaned as the severe throbbing on the right side of his head intensified. He wished a slow, painful death to whoever was making all the noise outside.

The opening theme song to *Star Wars* drifted out of his pocket. Jen. He'd set the ringtone for her weeks ago so he'd know without even looking if a call was from her.

Careful not to move his head too much, Brett pulled the device out. "Jen," he said, the sound of his own voice extremely loud to his pounding head.

"Hey, you. Are you not home yet?" Her voice seemed several decibels louder than usual. "I'm there now."

There wasn't a mallet-wielding idiot outside hitting a gong. The noise he'd heard was his doorbell. "I'm here. Give me a minute."

Brett let the cell phone slip to the floor. Slowly he swung both feet off the sofa and pushed himself up into a sitting position. For his efforts, the throbbing in his head intensified.

He moved across the room about as fast as a turtle going up a hill covered in wet cement but somehow he managed to reach the front door. Despite still wearing sunglasses, when he opened the door and light hit him, he flinched and touched his forehead.

"You not feeling well," she said.

"Migraine."

She moved inside and closed the door, once again blocking out the early evening sunlight. "C'mon, let's get you in bed." Jen slipped an arm around his waist.

At a different time, he would've had a great comeback to her statement. Tonight he was finding it hard to form simple one-word sentences.

With slow, controlled steps, he walked alongside Jen to his bedroom. When they reached it, she immediately closed all the blinds and pulled the covers back on his bed.

"You'll be more comfortable without this," she said, undoing his tie. She tossed it on the nightstand. "Do you have anything you can take for your head?"

Brett sat and kicked his shoes off. "No."

"Lie down and I'll go pick something up. I'll take your keys so I can let myself back in."

They only had tonight alone together. He didn't want to waste it with her playing nursemaid. His migraine had its own ideas though. "I'm sorry." He eased his head down to his pillow.

"No reason to be sorry. Rest." Jen's lips brushed against his forehead. "I'll be right back."

~

BRETT OPENED HIS EYES. The world around him was pitch-black and he was lying down. He still wore the clothes he'd left in this morning, minus his tie and jacket. However, someone had unbuttoned his shirt. Slowly, the memories from the last several hours trickled back to him. He'd come home with a migraine. Sometime after his return Jen had arrived. She'd helped him into bed before going and buying him some medicine. He remembered her coming in to check on him periodically while he rested, although he couldn't say exactly how many visits she'd made. He also remembered her rubbing his back while he lost the contents of his stomach in the bathroom. Afterward she'd handed him a damp facecloth and helped him back to bed. For all he knew though, that could have been five minutes or five hours ago. Regardless, he did know his head no longer felt as if someone was trying to split it in two.

Sitting up, he switched on the bedside lamp and checked his watch. Eleven o'clock. He'd been asleep longer than he'd thought.

The closing credits to the second *Lord of The Rings* movie greeted him when he entered the living room. All the lights in the room were turned off, but the television provided enough illumination for him to make out the sleeping form on the sofa.

Brett knelt down and ran a hand over her hair. She'd

kicked off her shoes but still wore her shorts and T-shirt. A half-empty bowl of popcorn remained on the coffee table along with a full glass of water. He suspected the popcorn had been her dinner tonight. He certainly didn't have many other options in the house. He'd been too busy to go shopping this week. Not that he'd been home much to eat anyway. He'd eaten at more restaurants and rest stops this week than he cared to remember. Since they'd planned to visit Tuscany, the Italian restaurant in town, tonight and then attend the fundraiser tomorrow night, he hadn't seen his lack of food as a big deal.

Jen would never complain about her lack of food choices or the fact he'd spent their one night alone together in bed. Still, he'd find a way to make it up to her. Eventually. Considering his hectic schedule leading up to the primary, it might be a while.

Brett slipped his arms under her. He'd already won the award for world's worst boyfriend tonight. He couldn't let her spend the whole night on the sofa too.

Jen's eyes opened before he could lift her. "Hey, you're up." She placed a hand on his cheek and smiled. "How are you feeling?" she asked, sitting up.

"Better." He moved onto the sofa next to her. "I'm sorry about tonight."

As he expected, she shrugged a shoulder. "No big deal. We'll have other Friday nights together."

He disagreed. "Yeah, it is a big deal. You came up so we could go out and have fun, not so you could act as my nurse. And then fall asleep on my sofa."

"Wrong. I drove up to see you, and I am seeing you. Besides, sometimes we all need someone to take care of us." She jabbed him in the shoulder "Even you, Buster."

"Buster? You can't think of anything better?"

"Maybe after you win the election, I'll change it to Senator Buster, but until then you'll have to live with plain old Buster."

"I guess that means I should come up with a nickname for you too?"

She considered his words before answering. "You can, but I warn you I have veto power over anything you come up with. So it better be something good."

"Don't worry, it'll be better than Buster." He moved in to kiss her but then remembered his mad dash to the porcelain god hours ago and stopped. Instead he kissed her hair. "I'll make tonight up to you soon. Promise."

"How about instead you promise to take a leave of absence from Homeland Security? You're stretching yourself way too thin. I bet you haven't had a good night's sleep in weeks. Between the hours and the stress, it's no surprise you got a migraine today. Keep up this pace and you'll probably be getting a lot more. And I won't always be here to take care of you when you do."

Carl had given him a similar lecture during their last meeting. The biggest difference between his and Jen's was the tone. Jen's voice contained worry and compassion; neither emotion had been present in Carl's.

"I'm thinking about it."

"Brett, I'm serious. Winning the election won't matter if you're too run-down to take office."

"I am too. I've been considering it all week. And you and Carl are probably right." Brett stood and held out his hand. They were both tired, and Saturday was going to be a long night. "Ready for bed?"

"Are you trying to change the subject again?" Although she hadn't answered his question, she let him help her up.

Another time he'd have to say affirmative, but not tonight. "No. I'm tired and you were just asleep. I think we both need some rest. But tomorrow before the fundraiser, I'll spend some time thinking about what you said."

"You do still look awful." She tugged on his hand. "C'mon, Buster, I'll tuck you back into bed."

∽

No MATTER the time or place, Brett preferred to drive himself. Despite Carl's suggestion he hire a car for tonight's event, he drove them into Boston. After handing the waiting valet his keys, he walked around and opened Jen's door.

"Ready?" He gave a slight nod to the reporters and photographers waiting outside the Harbor House.

"As I'll ever be."

"Just remember what I said. If anyone asks you a question and you don't want to answer, simply say you have no comment." He whispered the words as he slipped an arm around her waist. "I'm the one running for office. They can bother me all they want. They don't need to annoy you too."

"I think the media disagrees with you." She leaned closer when she spoke, her breath a warm caress against his skin. "I'll try not to let them bother me."

He didn't like it, but he knew she was right. "There won't be as many reporters inside." His press secretary had granted access to only a select number of media outlets, leaving everyone else to hang around outside for whatever leftovers they could get.

Several reporters called out to them as they walked toward the main entrance. He paused long enough to give a few short answers and tried to ignore the cameras around him. After all the media attention he'd received over the past few weeks, he had a better understanding of the hell the media regularly treated his family members to. Next to him, Jen remained silent, her back as stiff as a kitchen table.

"Mr. Sherbrooke, besides your parents, will any members of your family be in attendance tonight?" a reporter called out as they reached the door.

"Will President Sherbrooke and the First Lady be here?" another reporter asked.

He expected a few of his relatives would be here, including his parents, but he didn't intend to share the information. "I'm not certain."

"Mr. Sherbrooke," a male reporter called out. "Is Mia Troy expected? She was a big supporter of your uncle during his presidential campaign."

"As far as I know, she will not be here," he answered. "If you'll please excuse us, Jen and I don't want to be late."

The door opened before he touched the handle. The earpiece in the doorman's ear and the slight bulge under his jacket suggested he wasn't a Harbor House employee but rather part of the security team hired for the event.

His parents descended on them before they crossed the marble-tiled atrium. Lily Pierce, his press secretary, and Carl weren't far behind them. Both his parents managed only a brief hello before Carl reached them.

"Excellent, you're here," Carl said before turning his attention to Brett's parents. "It's nice to see you both again." Extending his hand, he looked in Jen's direction next. "Carl Filmore."

"Jennifer," she said, shaking the campaign manager's hand.

"Yes, I know, and later we should sit and talk. But right now I need to borrow Brett." Carl looked in his direction. "Samuel Castle is here and wishes to have a word with you."

Brett recognized the name. Samuel Castle owned not only a multinational food manufacturing company that had its headquarters in Springfield but was also the co-owner of the New England Rebels. Lawrence Castle, Samuel's brother and the other co-owner of the professional football team, had already publicly endorsed Vince Reed. According to Carl, Lawrence had donated a lot of money to his campaign as well. The two brothers were well known for sharing the same views, so Samuel's presence tonight made Brett curious. And while he wanted to hear what the man had to say, he didn't want to leave Jen on her own either.

"Brett, don't worry. We'll keep Jen company while you're away," Mom said, reading his mind.

He'd rather do it himself, but what he wanted wasn't important tonight. "I'll be back as soon as I can." Brett didn't care if there were people around them. He kissed Jen's cheek before leaving her in his mom's capable hands.

≈

SAMUEL CASTLE WAS HERE. She wasn't much of a football fan, but she'd heard of the man. Jen looked around the ballroom to see if she recognized any of the other society bigwigs. Immediately she spotted actor Anderson Brady, perhaps her only celebrity crush, standing alongside an older gentleman and an impeccably dressed woman. She smiled as she remembered her conversation with Brett about how she hadn't realized who he was when she first learned his last name and how she'd gone to graduate school with a man named Anderson Brady.

"Brett looks worn out. He's trying to do too much." Mrs. Sherbrooke's voice was barely audible over the hum of the other conversations. "Right now he needs to concentrate on the campaign and forget about his position with Homeland Security."

"Carl and I have both told him the same thing," Mr. Sherbrooke said. "Like with everything else, he's determined to do things his way."

The man's voice was so low she almost didn't hear it.

"Perhaps if you spoke to him, Jen. Maybe then he'd listen," Mrs. Sherbrooke said, including her in a conversation she wasn't sure she wanted to be a part of.

"I have, more than once, Mrs. Sherbrooke. And I think he might be coming around," she said.

He'd told her earlier this afternoon he planned to take a leave of absence from Homeland Security. However, she didn't think it was her place to share his intentions, no matter how much relief it would bring to his mom.

"His father and I would greatly appreciate any extra encouragement you can give him in that direction." She touched Jen's hand before she continued. "And call me Judith. Mrs. Sherbrooke is too impersonal, considering how important you are to my son."

And just how should she respond to such a comment? "He's important to me too."

It wasn't a lie, but it wasn't the whole truth either. She'd fallen half in love with him while exchanging letters. Since their first face-to-face meeting, she'd fallen the rest of the way. She couldn't admit the truth to his mother, especially when she hadn't told Brett yet.

"I assumed as much." The smile Judith gave her made Jen think the woman already knew the true extent of her feelings. "And I'm glad."

A warm hand settled on her shoulder. A moment later, Brett pulled out the chair next to her and sat. "Hope I'm not disturbing whatever private convo you two are having," Brett said as he put a hand over hers on the table.

"We were discussing how we all believe you're pushing yourself too hard," his mom said.

Brett squeezed Jen's hand. "No need to worry, Mom. I'm going to concentrate on only my campaign for now." He leaned into Jen's side. "And you," he whispered before moving away again. "I already let Carl know. Monday I'll talk to Homeland."

"Wise decision," Mr. Sherbrooke said.

An excited vibe spread through the room as the buzz of hushed conversations intensified. Jen turned to get a better look at the entranceway, hoping for a glance at whatever celebrity had caught everyone's attention this time. Only it wasn't a celebrity, at least not a Hollywood one standing there.

"Did you know your aunt Elizabeth was coming?" Mr. Sherbrooke asked.

"Last I talked to her, she wasn't sure," Brett answered.

Jen watched the woman under discussion cross the room, and the fact the First Lady of the United States was Brett's aunt hit her over the head like a baseball bat. Of course she'd known of the relationship for some time, but it had been an easy detail to overlook. With the woman coming toward them, she could no longer ignore the truth. The man she'd fallen in love with really did live in a world far removed from hers. Since he never acted as if he considered himself better than everyone else, she sometimes forgot that, but tonight the evidence was all around her. And for the first time since they kissed, she worried what it meant for their relationship.

On cue, both Brett and his dad stood when Elizabeth Sherbrooke reached their table. Jen guessed standing when a woman such as the First Lady approached a table was included on Jonathan Sherbrooke's list of things every gentleman must do. Brett still hadn't shared the list with her. Then again, maybe it pertained to all women. Brett had done the same thing when she'd walked in her living room the first time he'd visited her home. Thankfully, he hadn't done it since. It'd be way too bizarre and annoying for him to stand every time she walked in the room or approached a table.

"Aunt Elizabeth." Brett hugged the First Lady and then pulled a chair out for her. "I'm glad you made it tonight."

"I wouldn't miss it," the woman replied, her British accent still present despite the number of years she'd lived in the United States. "Warren wanted to attend, but it wasn't possible. He sends his regards."

Warren. Jen wasn't sure she'd ever get used to hearing people address President Sherbrooke so casually.

"Jen, this is my aunt Elizabeth," Brett said as he took his seat and once again slipped his hand over hers.

Brett's aunt turned her gray eyes Jen's way. For a moment or two, the woman studied her as if trying to peer into Jen's thoughts. Perhaps happy with whatever she'd determined, a whisper of a smile formed. "It's a pleasure to finally meet you."

Finally meet her? Did that mean Brett's other family members had spoken to the First Lady about her, or had she read one of the many articles published along with the photos of her and Brett kissing? Jen wasn't sure which would be worse.

"I look forward to getting to know you better this evening," Elizabeth Sherbrooke continued. "My son, Jake, said you are quite adept at keeping my nephew on his toes." A twinkle formed in the woman's eyes. "Between us, I believe it's exactly what Brett needs. Don't you agree, Judith?"

"Fully," Brett's mom answered.

Reading between the lines and making assumptions could be a risky venture. However, in Jen's head the women's comments were their way of saying they approved of her and Brett's relationship despite their different social backgrounds.

"I promise to do my best to keep him there," Jen said. Her statement earned her nods from both Sherbrooke women.

CHAPTER 13

PHILLIP FINISHED READING the documents in the file and closed it. "About damn time."

Ted had given him two weeks to uncover anything regarding Jennifer Wallace they could use against golden boy Brett Sherbrooke. He'd had his team working round the clock digging through everything they could get their hands on. Not a single person had found anything useful. Out of time, he'd been about to concede defeat and develop a new angle.

This morning, though, one of his associates delivered the file now on his desk. The information contained in it might be just the thing they needed to give Ted an edge. First, he needed to determine how to handle what he'd learned. Normally he'd outline a few ideas before deciding on the best one and putting it into action. This afternoon he didn't have the time that required. Ted was due any moment for another brief private meeting. Not long afterward, the rest of Ted's campaign team would arrive for a strategy session.

The office door opened without so much as a knock first, and Ted strolled in as if he owned the room. "Have you seen the latest polls?" Ted demanded, his voice vibrating with anger. "I was told you were one of the best." He dropped a stack of papers on the desk. "These numbers say otherwise."

Of course he'd seen the polls. Rather than the gap between Brett and Ted shrinking, it had grown larger over the past week. Phillip understood his employer's frustration, but the man only had himself to blame. If Ted had done a better job keeping his private life private, he wouldn't have such a sordid reputation working against him.

"I saw them. Don't worry, we still have plenty of time to change voters' opinions."

Ted ran a hand through his hair. "I don't share your assessment, Phillip. The vote is less than two months away."

To say they had less than two months was misleading. Technically they had six weeks and a few days until the primary, but considering Ted's mood this afternoon, Phillip wasn't going to split hairs with the man.

Without an invitation, Ted crossed to the wet bar and poured himself a generous portion of scotch. In one shot, he downed half the tumbler before refilling it and coming back toward the desk. "You've had your two weeks," he said as he sat down.

Again the man was technically incorrect. His two weeks had been up four days ago. If Ted didn't realize it, Phillip sure as hell wasn't going to remind him.

"Time to earn the money I'm paying you and come up with a new strategy, because you've obviously failed to find anything on Sherbrooke's girlfriend."

Phillip ground his teeth together and waited until he knew he wouldn't say something he'd later regret. "Actually, we might have found something. My associate delivered this earlier." He pushed the folder across the desk so Ted could read the contents and reach his own conclusion.

Ted flipped to the top page and started reading. "Interesting." He turned to the next page and kept going. He didn't comment again until he finished reviewing all the documents enclosed.

Closing the folder, Ted pushed it back across the desk. "You plan on using this, right?"

As soon as I verify the information and figured out the best way handle it, I will. Considering Ted's current mood, Phillip wisely kept the thought to himself. "Definitely, but we'll need to time it perfectly. For now let's keep this information away from the press."

CHAPTER 14

BRETT TOSSED his suit in a bag for the dry cleaner and left his bedroom in search of a snack. A full meal would have to wait until Jen arrived, but if he didn't grab something in the meantime, his insides were going to digest themselves. He'd had groceries delivered this week, so he had no shortage of options tonight. Having a fully stocked kitchen also meant he and Jen could stay locked inside all weekend and not venture out to any restaurants. The last few times they'd dined out, he'd felt as if they sat in a giant fishbowl. People had no qualms about watching them. They didn't have any problem approaching him when they were out either. If he was alone or with Carl, he didn't mind the unexpected interruptions. It was all part of being a public figure. When he was with Jen it was different. They had a limited amount of time together. He didn't want to waste it talking to businessmen or other politicians. When it happened, Jen brushed off his apologies and insisted it wasn't a big deal. He appreciated her constant understanding, but knew it might not last forever.

After he grabbed a beer, he raided what had turned into his snack cabinet. He'd loaded it with all his favorite junk food as well as Jen's so she'd have it when she came over. He'd even added several boxes of dog treats to the kitchen closet for Bo, who was another regular visitor. In fact, Bo even had his own dog bed in the living room now.

Tonight he pulled out the roasted almonds and tossed back a handful before he even closed the cabinet door. Brett washed them down before carrying both the beer and nuts back to the living room. While he waited for both his furniture delivery and Jen, he'd catch the baseball scores from today's earlier games. He had no idea how long he'd be waiting. Jen hadn't been able to tell him exactly when she'd get here. She and Kristen had taken their scout troop on a nature hike this morning as part of their animal habitats badge, whatever that was. She'd promised to come over as soon as they finished. The furniture company had given him a delivery window of between four and seven. So it was likely he'd have time to catch part of the Boston-Baltimore game slated to start at five.

Brett switched on the sports channel. Instead of the popular commenters being on the screen, an ad for Ted Smith greeted him. He ignored it and ate another handful of nuts while a faceless voice droned on about Smith's political expertise and stressed how tirelessly he'd worked during his time as lieutenant governor. The ad ended by asking voters what they wanted in Washington, someone with tested political experience or a novice. The question caught his attention.

Novice, my ass. He'd never held an office but his dad and his uncles had. He knew what went on both in the Senate and behind closed doors in Washington.

The doorbell stopped him from taking another swig of beer. As much as he wanted to see Jen, he hoped it was the men with his new furniture outside and not her. He hadn't told her he'd ordered the stuff she'd deemed necessary weeks ago, and he wanted to see the surprise on her face when she saw it.

Neither Jen nor his new furniture waited on the porch.

"Leah." They hadn't spoken since the fund-raiser in Boston, which wasn't unusual. He'd never been much for lengthy phone convos. "Come on in." He gave her a hug after she walked in and then closed the door. "What are you doing out this way?" For the past several years, Leah had called Connecticut home and, like his cousin Scott, worked in New York City.

"Tory is flying in for a friend's wedding this week. I'm meeting her in Boston. We've got plans for the night," Leah answered, referring to Victoria Sherbrooke, their second cousin and one of Leah's best friends. The two of them had been born two weeks apart and had roomed together at Phillips Exeter Academy in New Hampshire.

As far as far Brett knew, Tory still lived in California but made regular visits to the east coast, although he couldn't remember the last time he'd seen her. And he was okay with that. He'd never been close to her or her brother. Truthfully, he'd never been close to any of the Sherbrookes on the west coast.

"Courtney's coming with us."

He hadn't seen his cousin Courtney since his move back, even though she worked in Boston. According to Aunt Marilyn, Courtney's mom, she'd planned to attend the fund-raiser at the Harbor House but the flu had knocked his cousin on her butt. "Tell Court I said hi," he said.

Leah nodded and looked around the sparsely furnished living room. "Seriously, Brett, you need to do some decorating in here. I've seen patient waiting rooms with more character than this." She dropped her oversized purse on the coffee table. He never understood why she carried around something so large. The thing was big enough to conceal a twenty-pound medicine ball. "My offer still stands. I'll take care of everything for you, all you need to do is give me a key." She pointed across the room toward Bo's bed. "And what's with the dog bed? I don't see a dog. Do you make guests sit there?"

"Don't worry, I'm working on it." He loved his sister, but

he'd ask Jen's ten-year-old niece to decorate long before he'd let Leah do it. "The bed is for Jen's dog. She usually brings Bo when she spends the weekend. But if you want to use it, feel free."

"If even her dog has a bed here, you are in deep." She plucked a few almonds from the container he'd left on the coffee table. "Courtney and I were speculating who'd get engaged next, since her brother already took the plunge. We both thought it would be Curt, but if Jen's dog has a bed here, maybe it'll be you."

"I guess you and our dear cousin do need something more interesting than fashion to discuss." Brett waited for the reaction the comment would earn him.

"Oh please. I heard all about the betting pool Trent and Jake have going, so none of you are any better." Leah grabbed a few more nuts before heading for the kitchen. "I hope your fridge has more stuff in it than this room."

≈

SINCE A BRIGHT RED Porsche was parked in Brett's driveway, Jen pulled to the curb in front of his house. She didn't know who owned the car, but she hoped it wasn't Carl. She'd spent enough time in the man's presences at the fund-raiser to last her a lifetime. And that was saying a lot. She usually could tolerate being around anyone. Carl, though, had rubbed her the wrong way.

"Come on, Bo." She grabbed his leash and her purse. If Carl was here, she'd have to deal with it until he and Brett finished whatever issues they had.

She gave Bo a chance to take care of business before stepping onto the porch. The previous weekend they'd sat out there and enjoyed breakfast. She hoped they had the opportunity to do so again tomorrow, assuming the rain held off. If not, maybe she'd surprise Brett and serve him breakfast in bed. The man certainly deserved to be pampered a little when he got some downtime.

The front door swung open, and Leah rather than Brett greeted her. "My brother's upstairs on the phone with Carl," she said, explaining why she'd answered the door and not Brett. "I'm not sure how Brett stands working with the man."

She'd had similar thoughts herself. "Brett says he's one of the best."

"Dad says the same thing, but there's something about him I don't like. Since I don't have to work with him, it doesn't really matter."

Once again Jen shared Leah's opinion.

Jen walked inside and stopped short. When she'd left last weekend, only the sofa and coffee table had been keeping the silly large-screen television company. Now, armchairs and two end tables helped fill the room. "He got furniture."

Leah laughed. "I know. Really, it's about time. I was thinking about going and ordering it for him."

The gray leather chairs matched the gray sofa well, but they weren't what she would've picked out. In her opinion, the room needed some color. The walls were a boring off-white, and he'd never bothered to hang any pictures. The windows remained bare expect for the blinds, and the hardwood floors were beautiful but plain. She would've gone with some furniture in blue or perhaps dark purple instead. While she was at it, she'd also add an area rug to the room and some curtains.

"He even bought a kitchen table," Leah said.

"No way," Jen said with exaggerated surprise. "This I have to see."

"When they delivered the furniture tonight, I was stunned too. I can't believe it took him so long. He's owned the home for a year." Leah leaned down and scratched Bo behind the ears. "You must be Bo." The dog rewarded Brett's sister by licking her hand. "I saw your bed in the corner."

"I think he prefers your brother's sofa."

Brett entered the room and came straight toward her. "And the bed in the guest bedroom."

They had found Bo asleep in the room down the hall from the master bedroom more than once. Not that she blamed Bo. At home he slept with her, and a real mattress had to be more comfortable than his dog bed. Brett didn't give her a chance to comment or even say hello. Instead his mouth covered hers hungrily, sending spirals of ecstasy through her body despite the fact his sister stood in the room mere inches away.

As if from a great distance, she heard someone clear her throat. Then the sound came a second time.

"Hello," Leah said. "I'm still standing here. Can you save it for after I leave?"

When Jen realized Brett had no intention of ending their kiss even though they had an audience, she pulled away.

"You know where the door is, sis. Make sure you close it on your way out." Brett winked at Jen and lowered his lips toward her neck.

Leah crossed her arms and treated her brother to a glare capable of freezing a person solid. "I support your campaign and this how you treat me. Typical." Her frown faltered and a smile peeked out. "Jen, maybe you can finally teach my brother some manners."

"It might be too much of a challenge for me, but I'll do my best." Jen giggled when Brett tickled her. "Since I'm starving and someone finally invested in a kitchen table, maybe you can give me some pointers over dinner." Brett tickled the spot at the base of her spine again, but this time she swatted his hand away.

"Love to. I'm not meeting Tory and Courtney at Platinum until nine."

~

SHE GRABBED a pepper off Brett's pizza and popped it in her mouth. He'd left the food behind while he took another phone call from Carl. It was the third time he'd spoken with Carl since she'd arrived. Either the man didn't care or didn't realize Brett needed a life outside the campaign. If Brett did win the election, was this what he had to look forward to? Constant phone calls at all times of the day and night? She hoped not.

"He won't call again tonight." Brett dropped onto the sofa and pulled her legs across his lap again. "And assuming no other relatives make a surprise visit, we should be alone for the rest of the weekend."

Jen hadn't minded the visit with Leah. "I like your sister. She reminds me a little of Kristen."

He reached for his plate. With his sister over, they'd ordered pizza and saved the two filets he'd intended to grill tonight for tomorrow night. "She's got her moments." Brett raised the pepper-and-clam-topped pizza toward his mouth. "They are few and far between, but she has them."

His comment earned him a poke in the side. "Oh my God. You're so full of it," Jen said. "It's obvious you'd do anything for her. And vice versa. You're lucky to have such a great family."

Brett shook his head. "I plead the fifth. Should we put the movie back on?"

She watched his lips close around the pizza. The man really did have not only the most gorgeous mouth but also the most talented one. He could clear every thought from her head with a single kiss. And the way he made her body react when he used his lips on her breasts or anywhere else brought her to her proverbial knees every time. Even just looking at them now and thinking about how it felt when he wrapped them around a nipple sent heat to her core.

"Sure," she said in an attempt to keep her mind on something other than how much she wanted to tug him off to bed and have her way with him. While she planned on doing just that again tonight, she'd at least let him finish his late-night snack first. Jen hit Play on the remote control. "You know what this room still needs?"

"No."

"Curtains. Maybe a rug too," she answered, looking around the living room rather than at the television screen. "What do you think?"

Brett shrugged and reached for the second slice of pizza on his plate. "There are some in my bedroom. I got them this week. I just haven't had time to figure out how to hang them."

Jen knew he'd been out all week attending one event or another. "When did you manage to do so much shopping?"

"There's this great invention called the internet. You can log on and order whatever you need from stores. Then it gets shipped to you."

His comment didn't deserve anything more than an eye roll. "You ordered your furniture from a website?" She purchased everything from books to cooking pans on the internet, but furniture was different. Before she invested in a chair or a sofa, she wanted to sit on it, test it out and make sure she found it comfortable.

"And the curtains." He took a large bite of his pizza. "Ordered all the food in the kitchen on the internet too. The store delivered it right to the door."

Until the election was over, she agreed he needed all the help he could get when it came to everyday tasks. "I wish I lived closer. Then I could do things like grocery shop for you."

Brett set aside his plate and ran a hand up her thigh and under the hem of her pajama shorts. Her skin prickled at his touch. "I wish you lived closer too." His voice grew husky. "If you did, I'd have you help me with other things all the time." He slipped one finger under her panties and touched her. Desire shot through her and she got wet. "Maybe you can help me with them now."

He dipped his finger inside, and her muscles clenched around him. "I'm more than happy to help you anytime, anywhere." Jen sealed her promise with a kiss, ending conversation for a while.

CHAPTER 15

Looking away from the computer screen, Jen rubbed her neck, then answered the e-mail open on the screen. She managed to hit Send before yawning again. She needed either a good nap or a shot of caffeine. Since the workday had several more hours in it, she'd have to settle for the caffeine. Hopefully it would do the trick, because she had two important meetings to get through this afternoon. If the coffee didn't perk her up, she only had herself to blame.

Well, maybe she could lay some of the blame at Brett's feet as well. He'd arrived at her house well after nine the previous night. Then they'd stayed up into the early morning hours fine-tuning the speech he was set to give this afternoon.

Over the past couple weeks, it had become common for Brett to send her a simple hi or a thinking of you text whenever he got a moment's peace. The little messages always brightened her day.

Jen checked her cell phone now as she pulled her purse out of her bottom desk drawer.

Wish you were here, the message from Brett said.

She smiled. How could she not? The man was running for

the United States Senate yet he still managed to send her text messages.

Talk to you tonight, she typed before dropping the device into her purse. They might not see each other every day, but a night hadn't gone by this month they hadn't spoken no matter the time.

When Jen had sat near Eden, they'd developed the habit of always checking with each other before heading out for coffee. So rather than head toward the elevator, Jen walked down the hall to Eden's cubicle. She wasn't surprised to find her friend chatting away with a new employee Jen didn't recognize rather than working. Both women fell silent when Jen reached them.

"I'm going next door for a coffee. Do either of you want one?"

The employee Jen didn't know shook her head. "No thanks." She rolled her chair across to another cubicle without bothering to even introduce herself. Before getting back to work, the woman glanced back over at Jen once and then picked up her cell phone and started typing.

"If you were going to Ambrosia, I'd say yes, but I can't handle the stuff from next door," Eden said.

She much preferred the coffee at Ambrosia to what the chain coffee shop next door served as well, but she didn't have a lot time this afternoon. "It's not my first choice either, but it's better than what comes out of the machine in the break room."

"True," Eden said, as her eyes darted toward the computer screen and quickly back toward Jen. Definite concern lurked in the woman's dark eyes.

"Is everything okay?" Jen asked. "Do you need help with something?" It wouldn't be the first time Eden got stuck or fell behind and needed help to meet a deadline.

"Just working my way through these reports." She clicked the computer mouse and then turned her screen so Jen could see it. "You remember how tedious they can be." She gave Jen a tight smile. "But thanks for offering."

If Eden didn't want to confide in her, she wasn't going to press the issue. Everyone was entitled to his or her privacy, at least in her opinion. Thanks to firsthand experience, she knew the media didn't agree. "If anyone comes looking for me, tell them I'll be right back."

"Will do."

The usual office sounds drifted around her as she walked past the other occupied cubicles and offices. At first, she thought it was her imagination that each time she passed by coworkers conversations stopped and eyes turned her way. By the time she reached the end of the hall, she knew it wasn't. Something similar had happened right after the first photos of her and Brett appeared in the paper. Later the pictures of them attending the fund-raiser at the Harbor House together had intensified her coworkers' behavior. Over the past few weeks or so the looks had stopped.

At least until now.

Jen pulled her sweater tighter around her and entered the reception area. A handful of clients sat thumbing through magazines or checking their e-mails. Thankfully all seemed too preoccupied to notice her as she walked to the receptionist's desk.

"Oh, Jennifer, a courier delivered this for you. I was just about to call and let you know," Willow said from behind her desk, a large manila envelope in her hand.

Two of the clients reading magazines looked up in her direction. Jen did her best to ignore the unease gathering in her stomach. "Great. I expected them earlier, but better late than never," she said, keeping her eyes on the receptionist and not the sudden audience they had. "Do you mind holding them until I come back? I'm only going next door for a coffee."

"Sure, not a problem," Willow said.

"Thanks. Can I bring you back anything?"

"I'm still working on my iced coffee from lunch. But thanks for thinking of me."

Downstairs Jen stepped off the elevator and crossed the building's lobby. She caught sight of the media lingering outside before she reached the revolving glass door. Immediately after news of her and Brett's relationship broke, reporters and photographers had gathered outside the building, waiting to catch her. Thankfully, one of the building's security guards had shown her a back way out so she could avoid the media when she came and went. The door opened into the alley behind the building and made her walk to and from the parking garage or anywhere else longer, but it beat dealing with the media multiple times a day.

Either the reporters had grown bored or they hadn't found her newsworthy anymore, because over the last week and a half or so the number waiting outside had dwindled, allowing her to use the main entrance again. In fact, when she came in this morning, there hadn't been a single person outside.

The sidewalk out front now was an entirely different story. She estimated at least eight reporters were out there. She could also see a few news vans. For some unknown reason, the media's attention had been captured again.

Jen took several steps back and moved behind one of the decorative potted trees and considered her options. Going straight through the front door was out. Even if she didn't mind dealing with the reporters, it would take time and she was on a tight schedule this afternoon. She could go through the back door and into the alley, but who knew what might happen if they saw her walk into the coffee shop next door.

"Jennifer, is there a problem?" Aiden, the same security guard who had shown her the back way out, stood next to her.

She pointed toward the entrance and the spectacle gathered out there. "I was heading out for a coffee. Now I'm reconsidering."

"I don't blame you," Aiden said, sounding sympathetic.

"Surprised to see so many out there again. There was no one this morning."

"Me too." She couldn't for the life of her figure out why they'd returned. "I guess the break room coffee will have to do."

Aiden grimaced. "Hope it's better than what the machine in our break room spits out."

"Probably not," Jen admitted as she readjusted the straps of her purse. "But drinking it beats dealing with that." She pointed toward the doors. "Have a nice afternoon, Aiden."

~

BRETT HAD STARTED his day by meeting with the League of Women's Clubs of Massachusetts. One of the largest and oldest women's volunteer service organizations in the country, the group was involved in everything from supporting the preservation of natural resources to stressing civic involvement. Despite its lengthy and distinguished past, he'd never heard of the group until earlier this month. From there he'd driven clear across the state to Pittsfield. The event there had ended ten minutes ago, and he had nothing else on his agenda until tomorrow afternoon.

With a double-chocolate glazed donut and large iced coffee in hand, Brett opened his car door and got behind the wheel. Before he could enjoy a sip of the caffeinated beverage he needed desperately, his cell phone chimed. Brett tossed the bag with his sugary treat on the seat, took a sip of his drink, and pulled out the annoying device.

We've got a situation the text from Carl read.

Carl had sent him a similar text when the pictures of him and Jen first hit the papers. The man stressed about any unanticipated occurrence.

The phone chimed again before Brett responded.

Where are you? We need to meet NOW, Carl's next message stated.

At least two hours away. Not even on the Mass Pike yet.
Get to my office ASAP.

Carl never demanded. He suggested and sometimes tried to persuade, but he never flat-out made demands. The fact he was doing it this afternoon made Brett uneasy.

Brett started the car. Of course on the day a potential crisis struck he had to be on the opposite side of the friggin' state.

Be there as soon as I can. He didn't wait for another message. Tossing the cell phone on the passenger seat, he drove out of the parking lot.

Thirty minutes later, the music playing stopped and instead the sound of his phone ringing replaced it. The car's touch screen revealed the call was from his dad. First Carl, and now Dad. It couldn't be a coincidence. A crisis was brewing, or at least something they both viewed as a crisis.

Sending up a little thanks to whoever developed hands-free technology, Brett pressed the talk icon.

"Did you know?" Dad asked without returning Brett's hello.

"Know what?"

"How can you ask me that? It was the breaking news story on every station this afternoon."

Had his lead over Ted Smith taken a nosedive? Was that the major situation Carl needed to see him about? "I haven't been near a television all day. But I'm on my way to Carl's office. Whatever the problem, we'll develop a plan to handle it."

Carl was one of the best in the business. Brett had full confidence in him as well as the rest of the campaign team he'd hired. The situation would be resolved, and his campaign would move forward.

Silence came through the car's speakers. The lack of a response caused the unease from earlier to return.

"You really don't know." Dad's words were a clear statement. "Damn it."

Dad went out of his way not to swear. If he'd reverted to it now, the situation had nothing to do with the poll numbers.

"When you told me you'd known Jen for two years, I assumed you knew everything about her. Knew whether or not she was the kind of woman a United States Senator should be involved with."

"What the hell is going on?" Brett demanded.

"Evidently, Jen might not be who you think she is."

"Bullshit." As of late, he'd been vigilant about using any language that might offend or be perceived as crude. This afternoon he didn't care. "I don't know what's got you and Carl all worked up, but I know Jen. Whatever you saw is a fabricated story. Some stunt from Smith's camp."

Several seconds passed and Dad remained quiet. Finally he cleared his throat and said, "For your sake, I hope you're correct. I'll see you at Carl's office."

The call ended before he could demand more details. Brett considered his options. He could try Jen and see if she knew what the hell his dad was going on about. She'd still be at work though. He hated to bother her there. He could check the news feed on his cell phone. Doing so would mean pulling over. Rush hour traffic would soon descend on the highway and make his drive both longer and more frustrating. Stopping to read the news would only make the situation potentially worse.

Brett switched lanes and passed the driver in front of him. He'd have to wait to find out whatever shit had hit the fan today.

A three-car accident and the backup associated with it added at least forty minutes to Brett's commute. When he finally parked in the garage near Carl's building, he didn't bother to grab his suit jacket or put his tie back on. He didn't care if Dad would disapprove.

He had the elevator to himself for the ride up to the tenth floor. While he waited to reach Carl's floor, he sent Jen a text letting her know his call might be late tonight. The elevator doors opened before he got a response.

This evening Dee, Carl's personal assistant, sat at the reception desk. He'd never seen the woman seated there before, not even on the nights when their meetings had ended well after the rest of office had left. Instead the assistant always occupied her post a short distance from Carl's door.

"Good evening, Mr. Sherbrooke," Dee said, looking up from the project she worked on. She picked up the receiver on the desk. "Carl's in his office. I'll let him know you are on your way down."

When he went into a battle, he liked to know what awaited him. Tonight, he felt as if he was about to walk into the worst firefight of his life. "Dee, who else is here?"

Dee's finger hovered over a button on the phone console. "Only Mr. Sherbrooke is with Carl."

Brett didn't knock on the closed door. "What kind of situation are we dealing with?" he asked, walking inside.

Carl and Dad paused in their conversation. They wore matching grim expressions when they looked his way. A collection of newspapers and file folders littered the conference table.

"Good, you're finally here. Have a seat," Carl said. He picked up the remote control and muted the television. At the moment, a commercial was playing, but Brett had visited the office enough to know it was tuned to Carl's favorite news network.

"I assumed you knew the type of woman a potential senator should date. Evidently, I was mistaken," Carl said.

His grip on the chair tightened. It was the second time tonight someone had insinuated Jen wasn't good enough for him. He'd had enough of it. "Get to the point." Brett used the same tone with Carl as when he'd given orders to his men. He took the seat and looked from Dad to Carl when neither spoke up. "One of you talk. Now!"

"Smith's camp has uncovered some skeletons in Jen's closet," Dad answered. "They leaked them to the press today."

"Correction. They concocted some half-assed story about Jen and leaked it," Brett said.

Carl rolled his chair toward the opposite end of the table and grabbed a newspaper. "See for yourself." He handed it over.

The front page rather than the society section of the *Boston Times* featured a picture of them outside Peggy Sue's Café. It wasn't the picture or the fact it had been taken outside the café near his home that bothered Brett. It was the damn headline over it: Senatorial Candidate Brett Sherbrooke's Judgment Called Into Question.

His eyes drifted to the article beneath the picture, and he started to read. Nothing jumped out at him as anything more than the typical political mudslinging until he reached the fourth line. *Daughter of a convicted felon*, the sentence started. He shook his head and kept reading. The rest of the first few paragraphs detailed what a man named Dominic Russo had been convicted of and when. From there the story only went downhill at a breakneck pace. The last paragraph opened by stating that according to a relative, Jen had had her own run-in with the law, although it didn't go into any specifics. The article closed with the reporter not-so-subtly calling both Brett's judgment and integrity into question for associating with such a person.

Absolute disgust rolled over him, and Brett tossed the paper down. Political campaigns got nasty. It was all part of the game. Pure bullshit like this was way out of line.

"This story ran on every news station today and in all the papers," Dad said. "Even the *Star Insider* featured it."

Great. Just what he needed, to be on that trashy gossip show. "None of it's true." He'd met Reggie Wallace. The guy was a retired Army vet who worked as an electrician. There was no chance in hell he was an ex-con who'd committed murder or any other crime.

Carl leaned forward. "Brett, I know Phillip Young. He plays dirty and will stoop as low as he needs to assure his candidate wins." He tapped the newspaper Brett tossed aside with his index finger. "He wouldn't concoct a story like this when the facts are easy to verify."

"Carl's right. Smith's team wouldn't make these claims if they hadn't checked it out first. Information like this can be verified, and if it came back as fabricated, it'd backfire on them," Dad said.

He searched for another explanation because he couldn't argue with Dad's statement. "Then Smith's team got Jen confused with someone who shares her name. I'm sure there is more than one Jennifer Wallace in the United States. This article refers to a Dominic Russo. I've met Jen's parents, Reggie and Erica Wallace. I also know her brother, Keith, and sister, Kristen." Hell, he'd even met Jen's niece and brother-in-law.

"Phillip and his team would've made sure they had the correct person before running with the story," Carl said, shooting down Brett's argument right away. "My working theory is that Jennifer is adopted and whoever you met are her adopted parents. I've got people looking into it as we speak. But whatever you know about her, you need to share with us now. We need to start doing some damage control before this really hurts you."

Brett raked both hands through his hair and then down his face. Carl had a point. Jen could be adopted. He'd noticed the lack of any resemblance between her and the rest of her family. He'd ignored it. Not everyone looked like copies of their parents. Besides, it wasn't the type of question people usually asked each other, and she'd never mentioned it. "I don't know if she's adopted. It never came up," he said, wishing he did know.

"Like I said, I have people looking into her background as we speak," Carl said.

"Tell your people to hold off," he said. Jen deserved better than Carl's minions investigating her past. At the same time, Carl was right. The situation required a plan. "I'll talk to her and get the truth."

"Brett, let my team keep working," Carl said. "People lie to save their own skin. We have no way of knowing she won't too."

He knew people who fit Carl's description. "Not Jen. After I talk to her, I'll contact you. Tell your people to stop immediately. I'll get back to you tonight."

"I understand why you want to handle this yourself, but I suggest you reconsider. My team will be discreet and respectful. And remember time isn't on our side. If we wait too long to respond, the media might assume you're trying to hide something."

Damn it. Carl was right. "Fine let them keep looking, but don't issues any statement without my approval."

"If my people uncover anything, I call you before taking any action," Carl said.

Carl's voice let Brett just how much the campaign manager didn't like Brett's plan, but he also knew who wrote his paycheck.

"As soon as I get some answers, Carl, I'll call you. Before I go, is there anything else?" Brett asked. The sooner he got out of here the sooner he'd get some answers.

When Carl shook his head, Brett stood.

"I'll walk out with you," Dad said, coming to his feet too.

Hell. He had enough going through his head without a lecture from his dad. Unfortunately, he couldn't tell him to back off.

Dad waited until the elevator doors closed before speaking. "When this story proves true, what are you going to do?"

"If, Dad. If it proves accurate." Brett jabbed the button for the lobby.

"Brett, you've been around politics enough to know what Carl said is true. Ted Smith's team wouldn't have leaked this information if it wasn't at least partially true." Dad gripped his shoulder. "I like Jen. So does your mom. But are you willing to potentially sacrifice the race and your political future for her?" he asked. "You don't have to answer me. Just think about it and don't make any decisions until you can answer the question."

CHAPTER 16

JEN SPOTTED the news vans outside her house before she turned down her street. If they were out there, they'd bombard her the second she turned into the driveway. With a little luck, she might get into the garage and into the house. So far luck hadn't been on her side today. A more likely scenario would be a reporter would plant himself in front of her garage, meaning she either had to run him over to get inside or park in the driveway then walk the gauntlet of reporters to get inside the house.

Rather than chance it, she turned onto Hudson Street instead and parked in Anna and Billy's driveway. Their backyard abutted hers. Since they were on vacation, they wouldn't mind if she left her car there for the night. Pushing open the gate, she entered Anna and Billy's yard and crossed toward the gate in the fence, which would open into her yard. When she'd moved in, she'd found the extra gate an odd feature. Later, she'd learned she'd purchased her home from Billy's twin brother. Since their children had loved playing together so much, they'd had the extra gate installed in the fence so the cousins could visit whenever they wanted without having to walk far. Tonight the unique feature allowed her to sneak into her house without alerting the vultures hanging around outside.

"Hey, Bo." As usual the dog greeted her in the kitchen. After giving him a scratch behind the ears, she let him out into the backyard.

She'd been tempted to check the internet when the crowd gathered outside the office put a halt to her coffee run. She'd forced herself not to give in. Although she didn't know what had the media so curious again, she sensed it wasn't good. With two important meetings to get through, she needed her head in the game, not on whatever story the news was running. Jen had no good excuse for not checking now, other than she suspected she wasn't going to like what she found.

"Not looking isn't going to change it," she said, grabbing a diet root beer from the fridge.

Jen let Bo back in the house before retreating to her bedroom. "Let's see what the big story is."

The dog jumped on the bed next to her as she pulled up the *Providence Gazette*'s website. The headline staring back at her made her wish she hadn't: Brett Sherbrooke's Judgment Not All It Should Be.

She didn't need to read any further to know she wasn't going to like what followed in the article below the rather nice picture of her and Brett outside Ambrosia Pastry Shop and Café. Jen forced her eyes to scan the words anyway.

Jen read the first paragraph and stopped. Dropping her head in her hands, she tried to breathe as her stomach rolled. Dominic Russo. The name hadn't crossed her mind in a long time. How had they found out about him? As far as she knew, he was still rotting in a South Carolina prison.

She forced her head up and continued reading the article. It claimed, according to a relative, she'd had a run-in with the law herself. While the statement about her biological father was true, this part of the story sensationalized what had really happened all those years ago. Since the article had the facts straight about her biological father, would anyone believe her when she set the record straight on the rest?

Even though Jen knew she'd find similar articles on the other news sites, she typed in the web address for the *Boston Times*. Senatorial Candidate Brett Sherbrooke's Judgment Called Into Question, the headline on the site read. Although written by a different reporter, the article attached to the headline read similar to the one the *Providence Gazette* had published. She didn't look any farther. Instead, she closed the laptop and fell back on the bed.

The media was calling Brett's judgment and integrity into question? He was the most upstanding individual she'd ever met. The media shouldn't be holding her biological father's poor decisions against Brett, especially when he didn't even know the man existed.

Jen covered her face with her hands and groaned. His association with her could cost him the election, maybe even kill any chance he'd ever make it in politics. It wasn't fair. Especially considering the type of man he was running against. From the little she'd learned about Ted Smith, the man was an adulterer who made questionable business deals. A person with such low moral standards didn't have any place making decisions that would affect the country.

Bo nudged her hand, demanding her attention. Reaching over, she scratched the dog just below the collar, one of his favorite spots. "Do you think he hates me?"

She'd never lied to Brett. She'd introduced him to Reggie Wallace, the man she considered her father. Dominic Russo was simply someone she shared DNA with, nothing more. Would Brett see it that way? Or would he think she'd been trying to hide her true past from him? And if he did, what would he do?

Actually, even if he understood why she never mentioned she was adopted, Brett might not want anything else to do with her.

She didn't like it, but she realized there might only be one way for him to salvage his campaign, and more importantly his reputation. His family was probably already suggesting he end their relationship. She'd found both his parents, as well as the rest of his family, to be friendly and kind, but the Sherbrookes had an image to maintain. They wouldn't want one of their own dating a woman whose father had committed armed robbery and murder.

Jen moved into an upright position. "I better prepare myself now," she said to Bo. When Brett ended things, she wouldn't beg and plead with him to reconsider. Even though it would hurt like hell, she'd maintain her dignity. She'd reserve all her crying for the nights when she was alone.

Brett had said he'd call tonight, but considering this disaster, maybe she should try calling him now. She reached for her cell phone, but before she could bring up Brett's contact information, the phone rang and her mom's name appeared on the screen.

Something told her this call would only be the first in a long string of others.

"ANSWER THE DAMN PHONE." Brett paced from one end of the room to the other. Despite his command, the ringing stopped and Jen's voice mail came on. He'd wanted to call her the second he left Carl's office. He'd decided to wait. When they discussed the details of the article, he wanted Jen to have his full attention. He couldn't give her that if he was driving.

Suspecting there would be a media circus around his house, he'd gone straight from Carl's office to his brother's condo in Boston. Although the place was currently on the market, he knew Curt wouldn't mind if he used it for the night. He'd arrived there ten minutes ago and had been calling her ever since. So far she hadn't answered his calls or the two text messages he sent her. She was expecting his call, so why wasn't she answering or at least sending him back a text message? By now she'd seen the articles circulating. Even if she hadn't, someone she knew would've and alerted her to them. Was she avoiding him or had something happened to her? People got into accidents all the time driving to and from work. He'd seen one tonight on his way to Carl's office. If she was lying in a hospital bed, or worse, a morgue, she'd have no way of answering her phone and her family would have no easy way of contacting him. He couldn't call them either. He didn't have their phone numbers. Getting them might be possible.

Brett knew Kristen's address but unfortunately not her full name. Finding a cell phone number without a name would be difficult, at least for him. One of Carl's people could probably find it with even less information, but he had no intention of getting Carl's contacts involved with this too. He'd have to see if he could find either her mom's cell or home number instead.

He typed in the name Erica Wallace first. When all he got was an address and a list of possible relatives, he typed Reggie Wallace into the site. Once again, the website came back with only an address and a list of possible relatives. Apparently Jen's parents, like so many other people these days, didn't have a land-line, and finding cell phone numbers was more difficult than he'd expected.

Frustrated, he closed the laptop and tried Jen again. Like all his previous calls, it rang before going to voice mail. Although he'd left her several already, Brett left another message asking her to call him right away.

Brett dropped the cell phone next to the computer and considered his options. He could sit and wait for her to call back. If she was avoiding him, who knew when she might do that. And if she was injured and unable to call him, it might be days before Jen or someone in her family found a way to contact him. He knew her brother Keith worked for Elite Force Security these days. He might be able to reach him by calling the firm. It wasn't a guarantee, especially this late.

Waiting much longer to talk to her was out. He needed to know she was okay, and he needed answers. Brett checked his watch. It was already after eight o'clock. Leaving now, he'd get there around nine. Jen should still be awake, but they'd been up late last night working on the speech he'd given this morning. She might have called it a day and gone to bed already. If she had, he'd hate to disturb her. Unfortunately, he didn't see he had any choice tonight.

Brett pulled out of the parking garage and tried her number again. It rang several times before Jen's voice came through the car's speakers.

"Thank God you answered. I've been calling you," he said. "Are you okay?"

"Yeah, sorry. I think half the people on the planet have called me since I got home and turned my phone's ringer back on," Jen said, sounding frazzled. "I just hung up with Kristen and was about to call you."

Well at least she wasn't trying to avoid him.

"We need to talk. I'm on my way to your house now," Brett said.

"There are a few news vans outside. Most have left; I think they assumed I wasn't coming home tonight or something. Maybe the others will leave soon too. If they are still there when you get here, drive over to 8 Hudson Street. My neighbors are on vacation, and that's where I parked. There is a gate in the fence, and it will bring you right into my backyard."

He wasn't surprised the media was camped outside her house. "Will do. See you soon."

From the corner of her street, he saw the two news vans parked across from her house. Brett turned the corner and parked in her neighbors' driveway behind Jen's car. He followed her instructions and used the gate in the fence to enter her backyard.

He immediately noticed there was no light coming through the downstairs windows suggesting she remained upstairs with her blinds drawn so the media out front didn't know she was home.

The motion lights went on as he approached the back steps, and he knocked on the door. Bo's barking reached him through the door. Thanks to the outside lights, he saw the blinds on a nearby window move, and Jen peek out soon after. She opened the door a moment later.

"Come on in."

She took a step back so he could enter, and he gave her a quick once-over. She was wearing a pair of smiley face pajama bottoms with a matching T-shirt. Her hair was a wild mess, as if she dragged her fingers through it repeatedly.

He closed and locked the door. "Are you okay?"

"I've been better. The phone hasn't stopped ringing. After I talked to you, I turned it back to vibrate only." Jen moved across the room and sat. "How are you?"

"About the same," he admitted.

She nibbled on her thumbnail. In all the time they'd spent together, he'd never seen Jen bite her nails. When she caught him watching her, she folded her hands together instead.

He sat down and immediately Bo jumped up next to him. The dog didn't like to be left out. "Jen, we need to talk."

"I know," she whispered as her face dropped toward the floor. "But first I need to tell you I'm sorry."

Brett touched her face and nudged her chin up. "For what?" The only people he blamed for the situation were Phillip Young and whoever else worked for Ted Smith.

"The story in today's news, of course."

"Talk to me." He needed to know what he was dealing with. "Is any of it true?"

Jen sighed and sank back against the sofa cushions. "Yes and no."

He'd hoped for a resounding no but hadn't expected it. Carl

and Dad were right. Smith's camp wouldn't have released such intel if they weren't confident it was true. "Start with what they got right."

"The man mentioned in the article, Dominic Russo, is my biological father. I wasn't trying to hide him from you. I never think of the man, except when I get those family medical history questionnaires at a doctor's office." She paused and cleared her throat. "My biological mother, Tina Russo, died in a car accident when I was eight. She and my mom, the woman you met, were first cousins. Dominic was arrested about three years after the accident. He knew enough to give the authorities Mom's name as my next living relative. Mom and Dad took me in immediately, and as soon as they could, they adopted me."

"Russo was arrested for murder?" Brett had all the details from the article memorized.

"We were never close, even before my mother's death. At some point, he and two other men started holding up banks. I guess they did it while I was at school. I don't really know. Anyway, during their last attempt, a security guard inside the bank intervened, and Dominic shot him. They'd never hurt anyone before that day, so I think he panicked." She shrugged and reached over to pet Bo. "After he went to jail, I sent him letters for about a year. He never responded to any of them, so I stopped. As far as I know, he's still in prison."

He knew some people had terrible childhoods. Brett had never realized Jen was one. Despite the rotten parent she'd been born to, she didn't sound bitter or sad. Unsure of an appropriate response to the story she'd shared, he said, "I'm sorry."

"Don't be. From the moment I walked in the house, Mom and Dad treated me the same way they did their biological children. Kristen and Keith have always treated me as a sister. Regardless of what my DNA says, the four of them are my immediate family."

Not all children in a situation like Jen's got a chance at a loving family. She'd been lucky. "I'm glad you have them."

"Then you believe I wasn't trying to hide the truth from you?" she asked, sounding uncertain.

Brett cupped her face in his hands so she couldn't look away. "Affirmative." What the media and Carl believed would be another story, but he'd worry about it later. "What about the rest?"

"The part about me having a run-in with the police is mostly exaggerated."

Either you'd gotten in trouble with the cops or you hadn't. But he wouldn't jump to any conclusion. He'd hear Jen out. "How?"

She blew out a deep breath. "It happened about six months before Dominic was arrested. We'd moved to another new town, and I really wanted friends. There was this group at school. They were the cool kids. Everyone wanted to hang around with them."

He knew the type. Every school had them.

"In order to be in their group, you had to pass their tests," she said.

Jen reached out again to pet Bo. He noticed since arriving she hadn't touched him once. Usually when they sat like this, she'd lean her head on his shoulder or take his hand. Not tonight.

"There was another girl, Laura, who wanted to be part of their group too. Our test was to spray paint the shed behind her aunt's restaurant. One night we did it. Neither of us knew there were cameras outside. They captured us both on video. Laura's aunt, who happened to be married to the chief of police, called the authorities. They took both of us to the station in a police car and gave us a long lecture. Then I sat there until Dominic came and picked me up. I sat there for several hours," Jen said. "Thankfully, Laura's aunt didn't press any charges. I think she only called the police because she wanted to scare us. Make sure we never did something so stupid again. As a punishment, we had to help her repaint the shed."

"Yeah, I'd call that a definite exaggeration and not something the press should've printed." A new burst of anger exploded inside him. It was bad enough to drag up parts of her past that were true, but making a situation sound worse than it really had been and putting her reputation in question was unacceptable. "Other than the phone calls and the media outside, has anyone bothered you anywhere else?"

"Reporters were outside work again. And there were twice as many reporters when I got home then there are now."

Tomorrow they'd be back at her office and the number outside her house would double again. The media would get all they could from this story before leaving her alone.

"Brett, I'm sorry about all this." Finally she reached over and took his hands. "Even I know this can't be good for your campaign."

"It's not your fault."

He had the truth. Now he and Carl could develop a strategy to handle it.

"Your campaign is important. Do whatever you need to." Her voice cracked on her last sentence.

"I plan to."

He pulled out his cell phone and called Carl. The man answered on the second ring despite the time. "I'll be at your office in about ninety minutes. Have Lily met us there as soon as she can." He'd need his press secretary too.

Carl demanded answers, and Brett gave him the condensed version. When they got to Carl's office, he'd give him everything. "See you soon."

He didn't wait for a response before cutting the connection and calling Dad. His father answered faster than Carl had.

"Dad, I'm meeting Carl in about ninety minutes. Can you come?"

AND WHAT DID he plan to do, she wondered as she watched him make another phone call? After greeting his dad, he stood and walked away as he spoke. She followed him with her eyes. His facial expressions let her know he didn't like whatever his father was saying.

Brett raked a hand through his hair. "Enough. I'll see you soon." His voice reached her from across the room.

He shoved the device back into his pocket and looked toward the ceiling before rejoining her.

"More bad news?" she asked.

"Difference of opinion. It's not the first time Dad and I don't agree. I guarantee it won't be the last."

"You're meeting Carl and your dad tonight?"

"It can't wait."

He didn't seem in any rush to share his plan. If his plan included saying goodbye, she wished he'd get it over with and leave. "It's getting late, and you have a bit of a drive." She stood. "I'll make you a coffee for the road so you don't fall asleep."

"I know you've got work tomorrow, but I'd like you to come to my meeting with Carl tonight."

His words kept her from walking away.

Brett's request made sense. He wanted her to share the story she'd told him and answer any questions Carl or his dad might have. "After seeing the media gathered outside the office today, I told my boss I'd be working from home tomorrow." She'd hoped by Monday the media would lose interest in her again. Of course that had been before she saw the headlines tonight.

"Good. As soon as you pack a bag, we can drive into Boston together. After the meeting, we can either stay at a hotel in the city or drive back to my house. By then the media probably hanging around my place will have given up for the night at least."

"Do you think that's a good idea? If you really think I have to go, give me the address, and I'll meet you there. After it's over, I can drive home."

She didn't want to face Brett's dad, but she'd suffer through the meeting if it would help him. Staying at Brett's house or in a hotel with him was something else. If he planned to put distance between them, having her stay at his home wasn't the way to go about it.

He stood and advanced on her. "Why wouldn't it be a good idea?" he asked, but didn't give her a chance to answer. "And yeah, I need you there tonight. You might not be the one running for office, but we need to face this problem together."

"Together?" It didn't sound like he planned to walk away, but she didn't want to read too much into his statement either.

Brett put his hands on her waist and pulled her a little closer. "Isn't it what couples do? They work together? I don't have a lot of experience with relationships, but my parents always work as a unit."

Her parents did as well. "Yes, but I thought you'd find it easier to cut ties with me. You could go on record saying you didn't know about my past, which is the truth, and move on. If you did, the voters might not hold all this against you in November."

"Is that what you want?" He sounded concerned. "I know your involvement with me has turned into a major headache for you. Given time, things will die down."

She could say yes and possibly help save both his reputation and his chance of winning. A better person would do just that and ask him to leave. She wasn't a better person. "No, of course not. But I—" Jen wasn't sure what she planned to say, and Brett didn't give her a chance anyway.

"Good. Because if I had to choose between a seat in the Senate and you, I'd pick you every time."

Her mouth opened but no words came out. His admission

had robbed her of any intelligent thoughts. Before any came to her, he continued. "I love you."

Jen snapped her mouth shut, both stunned and elated by his words. "You... I...." She'd known he cared about her, but hadn't expected his feelings ran as deep as hers yet.

"This is the point when you tell me you love me too," Brett said before she could gather her thoughts enough to answer him.

Tonight the guy was a little too sure of himself. "Oh, really? You know what they say about assuming things, Buster."

"We're back to Buster again, are we? I still need to come up with a good nickname for you. I'll work on it." He didn't seem fazed by her comment. "And yeah, you love me. If you didn't, you would've kicked my ass to the curb the second the media started circling around. You're not the attention-seeking type."

He had an excellent point, and one she couldn't argue with. "At least on this, you're 100 percent right." She didn't want to stroke his ego too much. "Honestly, I was half in love with you before we met at Ambrosia."

"Same here." He sealed his confession with a kiss.

CHAPTER 17

BRETT PULLED into a spot and turned off the engine, not surprised to see Dad's car already parked further down the row. Except for his car and Dad's, this level of the garage remained empty. "Relax. You've got nothing to worry about."

She glanced down at her lap where she was busy picking her nails apart. "Easy for you to say. Carl works for you and this is your dad."

"You've met them both." If they were about to face a room of reporters, he'd understand her apprehension. Considering they were only meeting with Carl and Dad, her unease seemed unwarranted. "What are you worried they'll do?" he asked.

"Blame me for this disaster." She reached in her purse and pulled out her lipstick. "Not believe me." Jen tossed the tube back without opening it. "Try to change your mind about not dumping me."

"Neither is happening. I won't let it."

She offered him a weak smile. "Let's go, I guess. If we keep sitting here, I'm only going to tear off the rest of my nails."

The elevator doors opened, and they stepped out. "You should leave some stuff at my house," he said. He'd planned on telling her that and giving her a house key soon anyway; doing so now provided her with a momentary distraction. "Then you won't have to pack every time you plan to spend the night. I've got plenty of empty drawers you can take over. And I had a house key made for you."

"I will. You should do the same at my house," she said, her voice not much above a whisper as they approached the reception desk.

Once again Dee, Carl's assistant, was seated there instead of the receptionist. Considering the hour, he hadn't expected anyone to be here but Carl and Dad and eventually his press secretary. He should've known Carl would call his personal assistant in to work. It seemed no matter the time or day, the woman was at the office ready to do Carl's bidding.

"Hi," Brett said, feeling guilty about calling the meeting so late and forcing her to come in.

If Dee was bothered by the hour, she didn't let on. Instead she smiled and greeted them both. "Carl is in his office waiting," she said. "He wanted me to put in a food order once you arrived. What would you like?"

He felt bad enough without forcing Carl's assistant to get him food. Besides, they'd gone through the drive-thru at a fast food restaurant on the way here. "Thanks, but we ate."

"I have to go over anyway. Do either of you want coffee?" Dee asked.

Jen reached into her purse and pulled out her wallet. "Actually, I would love another." She held out a ten-dollar bill, but Dee didn't accept it.

"Don't worry about it. The office has an account next door," Dee said, looking at him. "Can I get you one, Mr. Sherbrooke?"

"Sure." As long as she wasn't making a special trip just for him, he'd have her grab him a coffee too.

When Brett and Jen entered the office, both Carl and Dad looked their way. They wore matching surprised expressions. He hadn't told either Jen would be joining them. Dad shook off his surprise first and stood.

"I wish it was under different circumstances, but it's nice to see you again," Dad said. He gestured toward the chair he'd pulled out. "Please have a seat."

While Jen got settled and exchanged greetings with Carl, Dad stepped over to him. "You're able to answer the question I posed earlier," he said.

His dad wasn't asking, but merely stating a fact. Brett answered him anyway. "Affirmative."

Dad gave him a curt nod as a response and then sat again. "We better get to work," he said.

Carl took the words as his cue to get the meeting underway even though Lily wasn't there yet. "I need to know everything, Brett. I can't come up with a good defense if I don't know all the specifics," he said, before he looked toward Jen. "I'm sure you've seen what the media is claiming. I need you to be honest with me. Jennifer, is Dominic Russo your father, and have you had problems with the law?"

Brett gripped her hand on the table and gave it a squeeze.

"Unfortunately, yes, Russo is my biological father," she said.

She didn't give either Carl or his dad a chance to question her. Instead she pressed on with the full story. And now, like he had earlier that night, he sent up a little thank-you she'd had the Wallaces to take her in and give her a loving family.

When she finished, both men asked her several questions about Dominic and her relationship with him.

"What about the other claim?" Carl asked, switching topics. "If you've ever had problems with the police or have ever been arrested, even if it's for something you did when you were seventeen, we need to know."

"I've never even gotten a speeding ticket."

Carl frowned. "I thought I stressed how important complete honesty was today. Jennifer, men like Phillip Young don't get their facts wrong," he said, and Brett considered the consequences of firing the man and walking out.

"Mr. Filmore, I am being honest with you. I have never been arrested." Jen's voice contained a hard edge he'd never heard before. She might have been nervous about the meeting, but she wasn't going to let Carl push her around. "If you give me a chance, I'll explain what incident the media must be referring to."

"I apologize. Please proceed."

The same hard edge remained in Jen's voice as shared the same story she'd told him.

"Not that it matters, but either Smith's team twisted the facts or Russo left some out when he shared them," Carl said once Jen finished.

"I'm surprised he even talked to anyone, or that he even remembers it happening." Jen said.

He hadn't thought about how the media got the intel. He hadn't cared. Jen raised a good point. Few people other than her and Dominic knew about the spray painting incident, so the relative mentioned in the article had to be her biological father.

Carl nodded. "I don't know why, but he did. I got confirmation before you arrived."

The why behind Dominic Russo's actions were irrelevant. "We need a strategy. Thoughts?"

Dad and Carl exchanged a glance. His dad seemed to shake his head at Carl but otherwise kept silent.

"Jennifer, would you mind giving us a few minutes alone?" Carl asked.

"Whatever you have to say, you can do so with Jen here." Brett didn't intend to keep secrets from her.

"Whatever you want." Carl removed his reading glasses and set them down. "You hired me to win. Your best bet for doing so after this is simple." He pointed to one of the many newspapers stacked on the conference table. "Come out and tell the public you knew nothing about Jennifer's past. It's not a lie. When Lily arrives, we can arrange for you to do a press conference. Then find a woman the voters will deem suitable."

Brett didn't care if Carl was right or not. "Not an option," he said.

"It's your campaign and reputation. How do you want to proceed?" Carl asked.

JEN WISHED she'd left the room when Carl asked her to. She'd expected him and Brett's dad to suggest he cut all ties with her. After all, she'd had the same idea. If she thought it might be the best way to save Brett's campaign, a man like Carl Filmore who ate and slept politics, would too. Still, hearing Carl tell Brett to find someone the voters would deem more suitable stung.

"Perhaps Jen should hold the press conference," Mr. Sherbrooke suggested. "She can share the same details she gave us with the media, and they can question her about Dominic Russo and the incident in South Carolina."

Mr. Sherbrooke wanted her to stand in front of reporters and television cameras and make a coherent speech. Her palms were getting sweaty just thinking about doing it.

"In the meantime, we'll contact the police station in South Carolina and try to find the restaurant owner. Someone down there should be able to corroborate the spray painting incident," Mr. Sherbrooke said, sharing the rest of his plan. "While it's not necessary, it won't hurt either to have someone who can back up Jen's statement."

She didn't love Mr. Sherbrooke's plan either, but it topped Carl's.

"Jen's not the one running for office," Brett said.

"Brett, you and I know it doesn't matter," Mr. Sherbrooke said, before looking toward her. "The decision, of course, is yours."

Brett turned in his seat. "You don't have to, Jen."

"Yes, I do." He was willing to risk his political future for her. The least she could do was face a group of reporters. "I've never done anything like this. I'll need some help preparing."

Mr. Sherbrooke's smile let her know he not only approved of her decision but also appreciated it. "Don't worry about anything, Jen. We'll make sure you're ready."

$\sim$

STANDING on her suite's balcony, Jen watched another group of reporters enter the Sherbrooke Regency Hotel. There had been a steady stream of news teams and reporters for the past hour. She shouldn't be out there watching because it was only increasing her anxiety level, which was already through the roof. Unfortunately, she couldn't seem to stop herself this afternoon. When she wasn't out here watching people enter the downtown Boston hotel, she was inside, pacing the elegant suite she'd been stuck in since leaving Carl's office late last night.

Carl, Jonathan Sherbrooke, and Lily, Brett's press secretary, had all agreed it would be best if she stayed where the media couldn't easily find her until after the press conference. Since it would take place at the Sherbrooke Regency, Brett decided they'd stay in a suite there at least until after the press conference. If the media did discover where she was, hotel security could keep the reporters away from her. Jen hadn't argued, not even when Carl suggested she not return home for an appropriate outfit. Instead he'd told her to give Dee her clothing and shoe size. The assistant had arrived at their suite with several outfits, underwear, and matching shoes an hour ago.

"I'm calling down for tea. Can I order you anything?" Judith Sherbrooke stepped out on the balcony.

She'd knocked on the suite door not long after Jen and Brett arrived yesterday, despite the time. She'd spent some time going over the best ways to handle the reporters today before leaving. Jen didn't know if Brett's parents had stayed at the hotel, but bright and early this morning, they'd knocked on the door and the four of them had breakfast together. Although Brett and his dad left not long after they finished eating, Judith had remained with her.

"Tea sounds great." If she was holding a teacup, she couldn't pick her nails again. They'd been a mess after breakfast, so Judith called the spa downstairs. Its manager had immediately sent up someone to give Jen a new manicure. If she ruined her nails again, there wouldn't be time to get them fixed before the press conference.

Jen expected Brett's mom to go back inside. Instead she remained outside and gazed down at the news vans parked down below. "Try to relax. You're going to do fine today. You're well prepared, and we'll all be close by." She placed her hand over Jen's on the railing. "Come inside. I'm still waiting to hear about how you and my son met."

She knew sharing the details wouldn't distract her from what awaited her downstairs, but it would help pass the time.

The suite door opened right after she told Judith about finding the picture of Brett with his two cousins on the internet. Brett and his dad walked in together. She hadn't heard from Brett since he left for Carl's office. If he was smiling now, their meeting must have gone well.

Even though his parents were present, Brett kissed her. "Carl's people located Debra McCormick, the restaurant owner, and her husband. He's retired from the police department, but she still owns Rustica." He sat in the chair next to her. "They both remember the incident and are willing to corroborate your story. Someone is with them now taking their full statement."

They had been located already? She'd only given the campaign manager the full story last night. Clearly Carl was one resourceful man. Jen was glad he was on Brett's side and not working for the opposition.

"Awesome." At least the media wouldn't be able to use one part of the story against Brett any longer.

"We need to head downstairs," he said, causing the butterflies in her stomach to grow extra-long wings.

His parents promised to meet them in the hallway and left the room, but Jen didn't move.

"Don't worry about a thing, Jenner."

"Jenner?" she asked, aware she was stalling but not caring.

Brett brushed his thumb over her hand, the slight touch helping to at least ease the anxiety inside her. "I told you I'd come up with a nickname for you," he said patiently, as if there wasn't a roomful of reporters waiting for them. "It's a hell of a lot better than Buster. What do you think?"

"I like it." She couldn't stall all day. "Come on, Buster. Let's get this over with."

Momentary panic swept through her as she watched Lily approach the podium and address the packed room. Jen didn't hear the woman's words until Lily said, "Jennifer Wallace."

When Lily said her name, it was her cue to join the press secretary. Despite knowing what she needed to do, her feet refused to move.

"You've got this, Jenner," Brett whispered. "And remember I love you."

EPILOGUE

DECEMBER, Election Day

IT'S ALMOST OVER, Brett thought as he checked the large television screen closest to him. The polls had closed at eight o'clock, and the final numbers were coming in.

Despite Phillip Young's best efforts, Brett had crushed Ted Smith in the primary and won the party nomination. Although it had been a tight race, Gina Hammond managed to capture her party's nomination in November too. Throughout the entire six weeks since the primary, Brett had been ahead by a wide margin. So far tonight's exit polls confirmed the data. Despite the optimistic intel, Brett wouldn't be able to relax until the final numbers were in and the race called. The unexpected happened all the time.

At that thought, his eyes settled on Jen across the room. She stood talking to his brother, just one of the many relatives in attendance, and Taylor, Curt's girlfriend. Jen epitomized the word unexpected. When they started exchanging letters over two years ago, he never expected to fall in love with her. Yet, it had happened.

"I still can't picture you on the Hill," Jake said, stopping next to him. Jake and his family had arrived in Massachusetts over the weekend, allowing them to spend time with Charlie's family and be here today for the election. "In fact, I'm not convinced we're not trapped in an alternate reality."

"I'm not there yet," Brett answered.

"Check the numbers again." Jake pointed toward one of the large televisions displaying the results announced so far. "Or do you need me to read them to you?"

"I've been reading them all night, but I'm not giving my victory speech just yet."

"Whatever." Jake crossed his arms and nodded in Curt's direction. "How much longer before he asks her?"

Brett watched his brother with his girlfriend. The campaign had sucked up most of his time, making it difficult to see his family. He'd managed enough time with Curt and Taylor though to know his brother would pop the question soon. But he hadn't discussed it with Curt, and his brother hadn't offered any specifics, so he didn't have an exact time frame.

"Within the year," he answered before he checked the data coming in again. According to the screen, he'd taken both Westport and Springfield.

Jake looked at the screen too. "Better have your victory speech ready," he said. "Anyway, I say Curt asks her sometime around Allison's wedding in the spring."

"I told you, you're wrong," Trent said, joining them. Trent and his wife, Addie, were both in attendance tonight too. "They'll be engaged by the New Year's Eve party at Cliff House."

If his brother arrived at the annual Sherbrooke New Year's Eve party engaged, Brett wouldn't be surprised. He planned on being engaged for the event himself.

"And the Senator here will be engaged in time for my sister's wedding," Trent said.

"I disagree with you on both," Jake said. "Help me out, Senator. Tell Trent he's wrong as usual."

An arm slipped around his waist, and he hoped Jen hadn't caught any of their conversation.

"Jake, didn't he tell you?" Jen asked with a laugh. "It's Senator Buster."

"I like it. Sounds dignified," Trent said.

"So, Senator Buster, who's right?" Jake asked again.

"That information is need to know only. You'll have to place your bet and wait for the results like everyone else."

Jen looked confused, and he didn't blame her. She hadn't been in the room when they'd talked about adding his name and Curt's to the pool of Sherbrooke men likely to get engaged next.

"I don't know what you guys are talking about, but Carl's headed this way," she said. "And he looks happy."

He'd never seen a bigger smile on Carl's face. The man was about to deliver good news. "I just heard from Kevin McGinnis. Gina's getting ready to call and concede the race to you."

JEN SIPPED her champagne and watched another group of well-wishers circle around Brett. Family members as well as campaign workers had been offering their congratulations since he took the call from Gina and then announced she'd conceded. He'd delivered his victory speech well over an hour ago. The celebration wouldn't be ending anytime soon if the atmosphere around her was anything to go by. Even if it went on for another eight hours, she didn't care. Brett deserved every moment of it. He, as well as his campaign staff, had worked nonstop to win, especially right after the story about her biological father broke.

Although Ted Smith had never taken a lead in the polls prior to the primary, he had temporarily narrowed the gap back in October. Thank God, it hadn't lasted. Brett insisted the press conference she gave and the statement from Debra McCormick and her husband killed any lead Ted had garnered following the initial story. Whether those things had helped or not, she didn't know. Either way, she was glad the media had lost interest in the whole topic. She was even happier her past hadn't cost Brett the future he wanted.

"When I worked on the Hill, I lived in Alexandria. You two should look for a house there. It's a great city, and the commute into Washington isn't too bad," Sara Hall, Brett's cousin, said. "Well, compared to driving in from other areas. It's still not a pleasant ride."

She'd first met Sara, President Sherbrooke's youngest daughter, at Allison Sherbrooke's engagement party. A woman well versed in politics, she'd made several trips back since then to help consult on Brett's campaign. Jen had gotten to know the woman well in the past two months.

"Are you going to move down when he does or wait a little while?" Sara asked.

They'd spent so much time getting him elected, they hadn't talked about what would happen between them once he won. Jen knew he loved her. Brett told her and showed her all the time. But this win and the move it required would add a new and unwanted challenge to their relationship.

No one appeared to be listening to them, and she trusted anything she told Sara would stay between them. "I don't know," Jen admitted. "He hasn't asked me to move down with him. Actually, neither of us has ever brought up the fact a win today would mean he has to relocate."

Sara looked across at her cousin. He'd left the previous group he'd been with and now stood with his cousins Derek and Scott as well as his uncles Mark and Harrison. "Long-distance relationships can be hard, but they're doable. Christopher and I did it for a while." Sara met her eyes again. "Brett won't settle for that. He's not one to settle for anything. He loves you. Before my cousin moves, he'll ask you to go with him. I suggest you start thinking about whether or not you want to go now so you're ready when the time comes."

If he asked, Jen already had her answer. She'd miss being close to her family, but the drive from the Washington area to Rhode Island was less than ten hours. A plane ticket to and from DC wasn't expensive either, so she could easily visit when she wanted. She liked working for Pattersen Financial, but she could find a new job.

"I've been looking for you," Christopher, Sara's husband, said as he and Brett joined them. "Why are the two of you hiding over here?" he asked, handing Sara a new glass of champagne.

Sara accepted the glass and took a sip before she answered. "I was filling Jen in on a few more of my cousin's faults. She deserves to know what she's getting, and I doubt anyone else has told her."

"Thanks a lot, Sara. Don't worry, I'll remember that and repay the favor someday," Brett said, before ignoring his cousin and her husband. "I'm sorry I left you alone for so long. I need a break from this. Let's go." Brett took the half-empty wine glass from her and passed it to his cousin before taking her hand. "Sara, if anyone's looking for me, tell them I'll be back soon."

"Since this is your big night, I'll do it. But don't make asking me for favors a habit, cuz." Sara winked at her and smiled. "Jen, make sure he comes back soon."

He'd already started leading her away, so she had to look back to answer. "I'll do my best."

Brett exited the hotel ballroom that had been converted into campaign headquarters for the night. He glanced left and right before heading straight for an elevator. When the doors opened, he tugged her inside behind him.

"I thought we were going outside for a minute." She watched him press the button for the eighth floor.

"Too many people out there tonight too," he said.

The elevator stopped, and they walked down the carpeted hallway. "I want some time alone with you." He passed the room key near the lock and pushed the door open.

Jen preceded him inside. Her eyes immediately settled on the suite's table. A bottle of wine sat chilling near two long-stemmed glasses. A dessert plate containing what appeared to be limoncello panna cotta with wild blueberry glaze sat in front of one seat. A large chocolate torte had been placed in front of the other. They were the same two desserts they'd ordered at Turin during what she considered their second official date.

She gestured toward the table. "This took some planning."

"Even if I didn't win tonight, I hoped to have a reason to celebrate." Brett pulled her chair out.

She didn't know how she should interrupt his cryptic comment. Jen sat and waited for him to explain as he poured them each a glass of white wine.

"Well, you did win, Senator, so we can celebrate," Jen said. "Congratulations. I couldn't be happier for you." She raised her glass and tapped it against his. "You deserve it."

He set his glass aside without tasting it. "I didn't ask you up here to celebrate my win." Brett cleared his throat and removed something from his seat. He stood there, his fists clenched by his sides, indecision on his face. "This might be clichéd, but it seems appropriate." He dropped to one knee and took her left hand. "Jenner, will you marry me?"

She'd hoped he'd ask her to move to Washington with him. She hadn't expected or imagined he'd propose before he relocated.

He didn't give her a chance to speak. "You can take as much time as you want planning the wedding." He moved the ring toward her knuckle even though she hadn't answered him. "But when I go to Washington next month, I want you to come with me."

Sara had told her Brett wouldn't settle for a long-distance relationship. She'd been correct.

"Getting a little ahead of yourself, aren't you?" she asked, unable to resist giving him a hard time. Jen pointed to the most gorgeous diamond engagement ring she'd ever seen. "Maybe you should give me a chance to answer you before you put it on me." Jen leaned forward and kissed him. "Yes, Senator Buster, I'll marry you and leave for Washington with you."

Brett kissed her, nearly turning her blood to steam. When he pulled away, he stood but kept a hand on her cheek. "You need to come up with something better than Buster soon, Jenner."

She raised her left hand and wiggled her fingers. "Soon I can call you hubby."

He smiled and kissed her again. "Can't wait." His voice echoed the same emotions she felt.

"Neither can I."

The End

I HOPE you enjoyed Brett and Jen's story. Be sure to keep a look out for the next Sherbrooke novel.

OTHER BOOKS BY CHRISTINA TETREAULT

Made in the USA
Middletown, DE
18 April 2019